S0-BFB-270

ROCKY MOUNTAIN ROMANCE

by

Anna Leigh

To Tatiana
Best wishes
AL

1

Anna Leigh

ISBN: 978-1-7321991-7-0

ISBN: 1-7321991-7-5

DEDICATION

For Christine
A strong, beautiful, and incredibly intelligent woman. You are a constant wonder and inspiration to me. You are amazing. I am blessed to have you in my life.

Anna Leigh

ACKNOWLEDGMENTS

No book can be completed without the help of many others, usually too numerous to mention all by name. Here are a few, and forgive me if I have excluded someone – I would write someone important, but you are all important to me.

First, my family without who's encouragement this would have not been completed. Especially my mom, who always believed. Then, to the group of reviewers who provided valuable insight and impetus for changing this work in ways to make it better, and to all those others for helping me to accomplish my goals –my readers who have made this effort a joy, especially Becky (no relation to the one in the book), Laura, and Bo for their assistance and support.

Finally, my gratitude and debt to the editor of this work, Jessica Snyder (jessicasnyderedits@gmail.com) who not only offered great insights and ideas to make this a better work, but also provided encouragement and praise.

Cover by Lizaa

One

Shannon Sullivan pulled her Honda Accord into the staff parking lot behind the university library. It was two minutes to nine, but if she was a few minutes late, it wouldn't matter. She was the Assistant Director. She pulled to her usual spot. There was a vehicle parked there already – a silver SUV.

"Dammit! I can't believe ..." Now she was going to have to hunt for a spot. She grabbed an envelope from the passenger side seat and quickly wrote the license number of the SUV. "As soon as I get to the office, I'll have that moron towed!"

It was almost ten minutes later before she found a spot near the student union. She decided that since she was late already, she'd grab a diet Coke in the union, then head to her office. Her mood had soured a bit from when she'd left home. Thankfully, the line was short. She got a fountain Coke in a paper cup and made sure the lid was on tight. Then, she headed to the library and her office, her feet making quick steps.

At 9:17 she arrived at the library and managed to get the door open. She walked down the hall to her office, trying not to let the morning's events put a dark cast on the day ahead. Outside her office was her co-worker and friend Sheri Chapman.

"Shannon! You're late!"

"Of course, I'm late, Sheri! Some moron parked in my space. All I wanted was a normal, routine day. I had to park by the union and now I'm going to call security and get the car towed. Probably some ..."

"No! The donation! This is the morning when that guy from the publisher is giving the library the big donation – AT NINE! You're supposed to be there."

"Oh, crap! Was that today?! No. Next week."

"Well, nobody told him. He's in the conference room with Lucy now. Lucy's called twice trying to find you!"

"Crap! Crap! Crap!" Shannon took off at a run, heading for the conference room with an armload of papers and the diet coke in her hand. Her calm, routine day wasn't to be. Worry filled her mind and there was this sick feeling in the pit of her stomach. *Where can I hide until this all goes away? God, I hope I don't throw up.*

Two

Will Daniels stood in the executive conference room with the Director of Library Services. He heard Lucy Crandall say, "I apologize Mr. Daniels. Shannon is almost never late. I can't imagine why she isn't here."

"Well, it's okay, Ms. Crandall. I'm sure something has happened to upset her normal schedule. It doesn't take much. I just hope nothing serious has happened."

"Lucy, please," she replied, smiling. "We could start without her, but she is really the best person to tell you about library operations. We really appreciate this kind and significant donation to our library."

Will Daniels turned from the window where he'd been looking at the Rocky Mountains only a short distance away. He looked at Lucy. She appeared to be about ten years his senior. *Blond hair, short, professionally done. Nicely tailored suit. Politically astute, probably – at least for the university setting. She's done well here.* He wondered why 'the boss' had picked this university in northern Colorado for a donation. Nobody ever knew.

"Well, I'm sure there has been some hold up," Lucy continued. "She's very punctual. Perhaps we should start the tour without her. We can catch up later – in my office."

Will thought there sounded like a hint of more in that statement than a meeting in Lucy's office.

"If you think that best. We probably should use what time we have."

Lucy ushered him to the door. "Let me get this, Will. Sometimes it sticks."

Lucy pulled on the door at the exact instant Shannon, on the other side, quickened her pace to shoulder through it. The door opened and a surprised Lucy and Will saw a redheaded figure trip on the threshold and fly through the opening.

No one was more surprised than the wide-eyed Shannon, whose natural instincts kicked in as she started to fall to the floor.

Her arm tightened around the folders, papers, and books in her arm. Her hand tightened around the diet Coke, turning it into a mini water cannon, spraying ice and ice-cold soft drink over Will from mid-stomach to mid-thigh.

Anna Leigh

Three

"Then what happened?" asked an incredulous Sheri.

Shannon was recounting her story and using a tissue she'd moistened with saliva to clean a small smudge on her shoe. "Then? Then, he caught me. Just before I hit the floor. I was all set to get the wind knocked out of me, and he caught me."

"Wow!"

"Yeah, wow. He'd just been doused with ice cold Coke. Right in his – you know. I'm surprised he could do anything but grab and curl. And wince."

"So?"

"So, after Lucy gave me a look that would likely turn mere mortals into ash, Mr. Daniels asked if he could have an hour to find a place to change and get into something, er, dry."

"You in major trouble?"

"I might be, but he made light of it. Lucy offered her office, and the way she did it makes me think she might be in heat."

"Really?"

"Yeah. You should have heard her. 'Oh, Mr. Daniels – Will – we can get your things for you and get you out of those things, wet things, and you can take my' – put a pause here – 'my private, um, office. I'll give you anything you need.' God! You could have poured it on a waffle."

Sheri giggled. "You sound a little jealous. What's he like?"

"Well aside from apparently having no feeling below the waist – what? Jealous? No. A nice guy, yes. Anyway, probably not my type. Nice dresser, though. Much better than the guys around here. Strong. He just caught me. And it wasn't like it was a problem. It was like I didn't weigh anything. He's handy if you happen to do something really stupid and almost – literally – fall flat on your face. God! What an idiot I am!"

"Could be worse."

Shannon stopped cleaning her shoe and looked at Sheri.

"How? Just how could it be worse?"

Sheri paused. "Figure of speech?"

Both women laughed.

"So, he's a guy who travels all over the world," said Sheri. "I wonder if he knows all the good restaurants in Paris. You'd like to go to Paris, right?" Sheri said the last while gesturing at the shelf full of books Shannon had collected on different countries and cities.

"My books tell me everything I need to know about all those places – even Paris – from the comfort of my own home, thank you. You can't get dysentery from reading these. And you can't end up in some hospital where you don't know what they are saying – much less doing to you."

"Not much of an adventure. He could probably make all that easier – and just maybe provide some additional adventure, if you know what I mean."

"I know exactly what you mean. After Robert, I'm not sure I ever want any of that 'adventure' again. Besides, I'm getting older. I'm not sure 'adventure' will come my way. Especially here. The students are young – too young. Everybody else is married or gay."

"Didn't somebody ask you out last week?"

"Yeah. I wondered if I should check his driver's license. Hit on by a child. Nope. I'd say even Robert was better than that, but I'd rather be in a convent."

"Speaking of Robert, I think he called your office earlier. You didn't answer, so he called me."

"What did you tell him?"

"You're not interested."

"Good girl. Now, I suppose I should go down to Lucy's office. I'm not sure I'm up to it. I just wanted a quiet, routine day."

Forty minutes later, Shannon stood outside Lucy's office. Her hands were damp and a little shaky. There was a small bird, or facsimile, flying around in her stomach. She was in trouble; she just wasn't sure how much. You never quite knew with Lucy. *I hope I don't throw up – especially after dousing the donor.*

"So? How's your morning going?" asked Lucy's assistant.

Smug little . . . thought Shannon. Technically, she worked for Shannon, but as Lucy's righthand – whatever – she was pretty much untouchable. Shannon began to say something not very clever in return, but Lucy's office door opened. The assistant quickly became absorbed in her work.

Lucy was holding the door while standing inside her office. Lucy's appearance wasn't what anyone would describe as welcoming.

Crap. I wonder if I'll get a blindfold and cigarette.

"Well, Shannon. We should talk about your – your tardy entrance earlier."

Shannon's hands got sweatier, and now there were apparently a flock of birds in her stomach. She started toward the door.

"Ladies. Good to see you again. And it's good to see you upright," Shannon turned to see Will Daniels smiling. "I hope you are okay after we opened the trap door on you."

Shannon's face was warm and she knew she was red.

"We were just going to chat about that – Will."

"Well, I have to apologize to Shannon."

"What? Why? I mean, not that I want to relive," Shannon searched her mind for a description that would minimize giving him an ice water bath.

"No. Really. I just found out that I stole your parking spot this morning, causing you to look for an alternate and making you late. The whole thing was really my fault – well, other than Lucy's perfect timing with the door. You two didn't practice that, did you?" he said with a laugh.

"It's just . . ." started Lucy.

"Please," interrupted Will. He placed his hand on Lucy's shoulder. "Why don't we say that none of that happened?"

Shannon watched Lucy's response to Will's hand. Lucy's eyes

closed just a bit, and lost focus. Her posture dipped, as if Will's touch had relaxed her completely.

Yup. In heat.

Lucy cleared her throat. "Well, I suppose. There's no benefit ..."

"Thank you." Will turned slightly, facing Shannon, out of Lucy's view, and winked.

"Well, let's go into the office." Lucy's office held a large desk. Two comfortable chairs faced the desk. Lucy took one of the chairs and directed Will to the other.

"Here, Shannon, you take this one," he said.

"You should have a chair, Will." It was Lucy, alpha female.

"No. No. I'm not going to sit while Shannon stands," he said while ushering her to the chair. Will sat against the desk. He was a bit closer to Lucy than Shannon.

My god! He's playing her and she has no idea. Shannon feigned looking into her purse to hide her smile at the thought.

Lucy appeared to be enjoying her close proximity. She leaned a bit forward and looked up at Will, her head tilted back. Shannon thought it the perfect submissive pose and didn't know whether she wanted to laugh or vomit.

"Well, Will, because of the earlier incident – she emphasized the word incident – our timing has been thrown off. We'll have to postpone to donation ceremony until after lunch. I have a meeting with the dean, then there are a couple of other things. So, it will be one o'clock before we can convene."

"Ceremony?"

"Well, ceremony may be a bit strong, but we wanted to have a few pictures and the dean wants to thank you personally. I hope that doesn't upset your plans."

"No. That will work out fine. Maybe Shannon would be kind enough to show me around to pass the time. We could grab a quick bite at the student union. Shannon?"

"Uh, yeah – yes. I could show you around the library and – we'll need to be at the dean's office at 1." Shannon wasn't sure just what she was going to show him, although she was upset with herself. Her mind was spinning. *I'm the Assistant Director of Library Services. Why am I flustered at a simple guided tour?* But it was clear to her, if no one else, that she was.

Four

"So, tell me about Shannon Sullivan," said Will. Shannon was sitting with him in the student union cafeteria, chatting over a small lunch.

"There's not much to tell," she replied. She sat forward, her arms on the table. She was close to him and took advantage of the chance to study him. *Nice looking. I like the eyes – pale blue – and the smile. It comes easy to him. Plus, he's paying attention to me.* Her face felt warm. She looked at the table top. *I can't believe I'm feeling shy – but it's been a long time since any man, well any man worth having . . .* Suddenly, she felt self-conscious and sat back, putting her hands into her lap.

"I find people are always more interesting than they believe they are. I'm betting you're the same." He took a bite of his burger, then a sip of his iced tea. *She's sweet. Seems so, anyway. Answers are straight forward.* He realized he was using the analytic interview skills he used with interviews of politicians.

"Well," Shannon took a breath and returned her eyes to him. She picked up her drink. She could hide behind it if necessary. "When I'm not trying to drown donors with ice-cold diet Coke ..."

"Please. I think we'd both rather forget that." He grimaced, then broke into a smile. Then, a laugh.

"I felt like such an idiot. First, I forgot about, uh, the donation." She dropped her gaze to the table briefly. "Probably not the best thing to admit when you're sitting across from the donor. It's like I'm saying the donation wasn't important." Her eyes returned to him. "Then, of course, there was the issue with the Coke. Not a good start."

"You're recovering pretty well. Tell me about your history. How did you become the assistant director here?"

"I grew up a few miles south of here – in Windsor." There was his smile again. And, his eyes were fixed on hers. Her face was warm again. She looked at the tabletop then back at him. "I did okay in school, but money was in short supply. I decided to go to college here. It allowed me to live at home, save some money on expenses. I got my Bachelor's and was studying for my Master's in library science when a job came open at the library. So, I was able to get paid for what I was studying and take advantage of cheaper tuition for employees. Win. Win. Win. After a few years, I found myself working in more responsible positions until I was promoted to Assistant Director. Lucy does all of the strategic stuff. I take care of everything not strategic."

"So, you're the operations officer."

"The what?"

"Operations officer. Basically, responsible for making sure everything runs."

"That's me."

"Sounds like a big job. A lot of responsibility."

"I can handle it."

"No doubt. I didn't want to make it sound like I thought you couldn't. You think you'll take over the Director's spot someday?"

"I'm afraid that Lucy will be in that chair until the sun burns out or maybe if she becomes a dean. Unless somebody comes along, sweeps her off her feet, and takes her away from here. Don't suppose you'd be willing to do that."

"Uh, no. Why even ask?"

"The way she melted when you 'played' her in the office. Anyway, tell me about Will Daniels, rich donor and library director whisperer," she said with a smile.

"I hate to spoil your illusion, but I'm not the rich donor. The rich donor, the CEO, is somewhat of a recluse. He isn't seen much. Nobody knows for sure how he picks the places he donates to, but he usually has someone deliver the donation. In this case, me."

"Then, what do you usually do?" she asked.

"I'm a journalist. I write stories. They get published."

"Kinda short bio, isn't it?"

"Okay, I was born and raised near St. Louis." Then, it hit him. *Why didn't I see it before? Something in her eyes. Same trusting nature.* Warmth and sadness suddenly filled him. He realized that he'd paused longer than he should have. "Uh, I spent a few years in the military. When I got out, I attended Washington University. St. Louis, not Washington State; it's a common mistake. Got a Bachelor's in journalism. I got a job with a small paper, then a larger one. One day, I was approached to work for a company that has multiple magazines and a news service. The money was good. I get to travel. I'll have to admit, I'm enjoying life."

"No Mrs. Daniels or future Mrs. Daniels? Don't get me wrong. I just want to be ahead of the game so I can enjoy Lucy's response when she finds out."

Shannon saw his face darken for just a moment. He paused, then, "No. Neither. I travel too much right now. My job is my life." He paused again. "But back to Shannon Sullivan. Just a few questions to satisfy my innate curiosity – okay?"

"O-k-a-y," Shannon responded a little warily.

"Pick one. Cake or ice cream?"

"Really? Ice cream. Especially if it is on a big piece of cake."

"Mountains or sea shore?"

"Duh! Rocky Mountains – just about a stone's throw away. You might have noticed them out the window." She was laughing.

"Oh, yeah, right. So, I guess books or movies would be a stupid question."

"You don't know until you ask."

"Okay, books or movies?"

"Duh! Books, of course. Where do I work?" By now both were laughing.

Will looked at is watch. "Looks like time to head to the dean's office. We'll have to continue this later. Maybe I can find a way to get you back."

They stood and set their trays in the dish return. Will paused and picked up a small paper from a stack. "School paper?"

"Yeah. Like most, it's a weekly. Sometimes the news is a little thin," she said.

"That must be why they have a story on a motorcycle jump

gone bad – from ten years ago."

"Yeah. The guy screwed up and fell short of the other side. Two weeks in the hospital. Lucky he wasn't killed."

"Yeah," he said quietly. He seemed to be lost in the story.

They walked to the dean's office in silence. The ceremony, as it was, turned out to be mercifully short. Will was happy to have it over in less than ten minutes. The only people attending were the dean, Lucy, Shannon, and a photographer/journalist for the school paper who shot three pictures and took a few notes for the next week's article.

Lucy, Shannon, and Will walked back to the library together.

"So, Will," Lucy asked, "I suppose you'll be in a hurry to get home to your family."

"Uh, no. I don't have a family to get home to."

Shannon was busy staring sideways at the campus while trying to hide a wide grin.

"Oh?" said Lucy. "No one special?" There was a hint of what Shannon thought was hope in Lucy's voice.

"No. Not at the moment."

"Well, if you're going to be here for another day or two, maybe we could have dinner – tonight?"

Will was trying to figure out a way to decline gracefully, but nothing was coming to him. "Um."

"Why don't you just come over to my place? I'm a decent cook. I'll fix you something you couldn't get in a restaurant. Besides, you must be tired of eating in restaurants all the time."

Shannon was working hard not to laugh out loud while she envisioned Lucy ripping Will's clothes off. *Something he couldn't get in a restaurant – not without being arrested, that is. She'd love to fix him Lucy au natural – with all the fixin's. Maybe there will be wedding bells and I'll get to be director after all. Still, I'd hate to sacrifice him. He seems decent enough.*

"Gosh, Lucy," interrupted Shannon, "Will must have forgotten that he and I were going to go over some things this afternoon –

information for his boss, the actual donor – and it will likely run into dinner. Will?"

"Uh, right. I'd almost forgotten, the ceremony and all. I'll have to take a rain check, Lucy."

"Oh, okay." Lucy was mildly dejected.

They arrived at the library. Lucy headed for a meeting. Will asked Shannon if he could use the second room in her office to check something on his computer. How could she refuse? "Sure. But you owe me," she said.

"I owe you?"

"Yes. Much as I'd like to see Lucy ensnare somebody, you seem like a nice enough guy. I saved you. You owe me."

"I'll try to find some way to make it up to you."

"Well, for starters, you're probably on the hook for dinner," she replied, smiling, "after we fake going over some reports until Lucy leaves."

"I will be my pleasure, he said returning her smile, then added, "the dinner, I'm not sure about staring at reports."

She saw him looking at her longer than she thought normal. He had a strange expression. It didn't matter. She suddenly decided she liked him looking at her.

Five

Will went into a small secondary room behind Shannon's main office. It was used as a library, of sorts, to store documents important to the operation of the library. It also had a small desk. Will had retrieved his laptop and set it up, out of sight.

He returned to her outer office. "I've got to make a call to my office."

"Do you want me to leave?"

"No. I'm not going to kick you out of your own office. I just wanted you to know. I don't want to disturb you."

"No problem."

Will returned to the small office and punched the office number into his mobile phone.

"International News Service. This is Alexa. How may I direct your call?"

"Hi Alexa. It's Will. Can I talk to the boss?"

"Oh, hi Will! Let me check." There was a pause.

"Will? How's the trip? The check cleared, didn't it?" There was a chuckle on the other end of the line.

"Yeah, no problem."

"So, what's up. I know with you; it has to be business. You've got to learn to relax; take time off. We sent you there to force you to relax, you know."

"Hey. I love my work. More than laying around some beach doing nothing. Anyway, I stumbled onto something. I'd like to take a couple of days to see if there is any story. I can use vacation time, if you want."

"What's the story?"

"Maybe nothing, but mostly I get the feeling there's something just not right. I'll send you the information."

"Okay. Don't worry about using vacation time. You never take any – must have a couple of years' worth built up. Keep me advised. Your instincts are usually pretty good."

Will punched off. He leaned back in his chair. He could just see Shannon's back – she was sitting at her desk. A pale freckled hand moved her red hair around to her back. *Beautiful young woman – like the girl-next-door that makes your mouth drop open. A memory of his teen years came to mind. Then disappeared. Ariel's image appeared in his mind. How happy they'd been. Then, then she was gone. Taken. After that, there was only work. Work didn't rip your heart out.*

He picked up the paper and reread the story on the motor-cycle jump.

Six

Shannon logged onto her computer. Her office door opened.

"So. Who was the guy you were with in the cafeteria?"

"Robert. What are you doing here?"

"I'm allowed. Student and part-time employee and all. Who was the guy? You seemed to be pretty chummy – laughing and all." There was an edge to his voice.

"He's a donor. Not that it is any of your business. Why do you care?"

"Because I *make* it my business when some guy is around my girl."

"I'm not *your girl*, Robert. We're done. We're over. We've been over."

"You say that, but we're only over because you don't realize your place is with me. Once you understand that and acknowledge that, you'll see. We're not over."

"*Get out, Robert.* Get out and don't come back. Or I'll call security and report you to HR."

"This isn't over Shannon. We're going to be together. You'll see."

"*Get out!*"

Robert left the office, looking over his shoulder and scowling as the door closed.

Shannon's hands were shaking and her face was hot. She knew she was red. She was both mad and shaken.

Will appeared out of the small room. "Sounds serious."

"That's history. We're done." She stuffed her hands into her pockets to hide the shaking. The heat in her face receded.

"Doesn't sound like he thinks you're done. Sounds pretty scary, if you ask me."

"Well, Robert was always pretty possessive. I think he thinks he gets what he wants. Thing is, and I probably shouldn't say this, but at first, he seemed to be a good guy. Well, decent, anyway. But he was into what he was into. I was like an accessory. Didn't matter what I wanted. Just what he wanted. I was his arm candy – not that I'm actually arm candy material."

"Don't sell yourself short. You're a beautiful young woman."

Shannon felt the heat return to her face. The reason was different. She looked at Will. It was like seeing him for the first time. Light brown hair and blue eyes. His eyes were penetrating, hypnotic and seemed to tell her it was more than small talk. He was concerned. Her pulse picked up and she could feel it in her chest. She averted her eyes from his at the thought. There was a connection somewhere that she wasn't sure she was ready for. "No need. Anyway, if he wanted to get rid of me, he would be fine with it – well, he'd be telling stories about what a miserable person I am and how he couldn't stand me anymore. But the fact that I left him ..."

"He thinks he owns you. And that's dangerous. You shouldn't minimize it. He threatened you." There was a protective feeling within him. It was growing.

"I don't think it's quite that bad. Besides, you can't worry about me. You may have escaped Lucy's lair for the time being. I just about lost it when she asked you to her place. Again, you owe me. Still, I was hoping for a June wedding for her and a new office for me. Hate to throw you to the wolves, but ..."

"Thanks. I wouldn't take Robert lightly."

Shannon left her office and walked across the hall to Sheri's office. Her head was on a swivel. She didn't want to admit it, but Robert had shaken her. Sheri was on the phone but ended the call shortly after Shannon entered.

"What's up?"

"Robert came in."

"You haven't seen him in a while. What did he want? I assume he wasn't there to give you anything. He was a taker. He never gave."

"I guess he saw me in the student union with Will Daniels. We were having a bit to eat before the big ceremony – you know all four of us, including the photographer – in the dean's office. He wanted to know who 'the guy' was."

"Really?"

"Yeah. He got kind of ugly, too. Says I'm still 'his girl,' no matter what I think."

"*That's* scary!"

"Will was in the back room, out of sight when it happened. He said the same thing. I tried to play it down, but I have to admit, it scared me a little, too."

"A little?"

"Well, maybe more than a little. I'm not quite sure what to do."

"What did Will say?"

"He said I should take it seriously. I'm not sure how to do that without making major trouble for Robert. And I don't think that will make the situation any better. But, on a completely different subject, Lucy asked Will to dinner tonight. She wanted him to come to her place so she could, how did she put it, 'I'll fix you something you couldn't get in a restaurant.' I can almost hear the multiple locks on her door, closing him in." The tension relaxed and both women were laughing. "I bailed him out. Pretended we have to work. I hope there isn't too much retribution – you know, Hurricane Lucy."

"Wouldn't make her any happier to deal with around here. We could check with ROTC and see if we could borrow a couple helmets and flak jackets." Sheri paused. "Maybe you should get them because of Robert."

"Robert is a jerk, but I can't believe he'd actually hurt me."

"But you said that before you left, he was acting out if you couldn't – or didn't – do what was on his agenda. You, know slamming doors."

"Yeah. The last straw was when he punched the wall hard enough to put a hole in the drywall. I figured that wasn't a good sign and decided it was time to go. But I thought after six months – no, wait, it's been eight – he would have moved on."

"Well, if you ask me, you need to do something – something concrete – to show him that he's no longer on your agenda."

"Well, if you get any ideas about what that might be – without making everything worse – let me know."

Shannon walked back to her office. For the time being, she decided she wouldn't tell Sheri about her libido running somewhat amok during her conversation with Will.

Seven

The sign on the door read Arbo's – Authentic American Fusion Cuisine. Will wasn't sure what American fusion was, much less authentic American fusion. Maybe hush puppies with your clam chowder.

"This place is really hard to get into," said Shannon. "How did you get reservations?"

"I made a few calls. Told a few lies. Probably better if you didn't know." Truth was, he'd called a friend who called the restaurant – from New York – letting them in on a little 'secret.' A food critic was going to visit the restaurant to do a review. The friend let them know who the 'critic' was, and when Will called, voila, a table appeared. The friend even told them what kind of table the critic liked – out of the way, window okay. Something quiet, but not romantic. Will had done this on a few occasions for business. Even so, he always felt a little guilty.

They were shown to their table by the maître d'. A nice little table, almost in the corner, next to the window.

"I hope you will enjoy our little restaurant. We strive to make all our guests feel the specialness of the dining experience."

Will held Shannon's chair. She tried to look nonchalant, but her previous dates never thought to do that.

Will took his seat, directly across.

The waiter appeared almost immediately with two small cups of red liquid. The waiter described the special treat – complementary, of course – in detail. Will thanked him.

"Yes. Very nice." Will smiled. It was a basic gazpacho soup – Andalusian, that is, Spanish, rather than American. And, it had been run through a blender to smooth the consistency.

They perused the menus. "What looks good to you, Shannon?"

She smiled. "I wonder if the fish is fresh. Wait! There aren't any prices. How will we know ..."

"It's known as a lady's menu. So, the lady wouldn't worry about the cost of whatever she was ordering. Kind of went out of style some time ago."

Will glanced in the direction of the waiter. "The lady was wondering if the fish is fresh."

"But of course. The Dover sole was flown in fresh this morning – Dover, England, of course."

"Of course."

"The cod, as well, from the Atlantic."

"Well thank you."

"Would you like to order now? Madame?" asked the waiter.

"Yes. Thank you. I believe I will have the Dover sole and the fresh dandelion greens."

"Very good, Madame. And for you, sir?"

"I also would like the Dover sole. I'd like to start with the arugula and fresh berries salad. Oh, yes, a bottle of Sancerre, if you would be so kind."

"Certainly, Sir. And may I say, a perfect choice."

"Thank you."

The waiter disappeared and the wine steward appeared almost immediately with the wine. It was a nice year and estate. Will made a bit of a show during the tasting – if nothing else to keep up with the charade of being a food and wine snob.

"Well," said Shannon after her first sip. "This is a lovely wine." She held her glass up and Will touched his to hers.

Will smiled. Shannon's red hair flowed down onto her shoulders. She had pale skin and freckles. There was something about her presence that made him feel warm.

His reverie was broken when she said, "So, can I have a little more extended version of your bio?"

"What?"

"A bit more bio, please. After all, here we are at dinner. I should know something about the gentleman with whom I am dining."

"With whom? Yikes! Okay, but then, I get a bit more on you.

Deal?" Will didn't wait for a reply. "I was born and raised in St. Charles, Missouri – it's across the Missouri River from St. Louis. Played some sports in high school; track and wrestling, and graduated with respectable grades. I worked for a printer for a short time after graduation, then decided I needed a change. I joined the Air Force and ended up in security. I did pretty well, then was accepted in pararescue, guys who rescue and treat downed pilots – as well as some other things. I liked that, but I was asked to do additional security work. After eight years, I got out and went to Washington University. I got a degree in journalism and graduated with decent, not spectacular grades. I got a job on a small paper, then a slightly bigger one. Then I was asked to interview for this job."

"I assume you like this job."

"No. I love this job. I get to travel the world, live in different places while I research the stories, and pretty much get to do the stories I want."

"Doesn't sound like you have much of a home life," she said.

"Home life? No." Again, he seemed to darken for a bit. "I've got a small apartment in Paris – the fifth arrondissement – but I don't spend much time there. Like Willie Nelson said in the song, 'Life, my love, is making music with my friends, and I can't wait to get on the road again.' Only for me it is the pursuit of the story. I'm afraid that doesn't lend itself to much of a home life."

Shannon's heart sank. She didn't know why. Will was here for one or two days – to deliver a check. Then, he would be gone. There was no reason to feel a sense of loss. And yet, there was a sad, empty feeling.

She was startled when he said, "And you?" Although he seemed muted.

"Huh? Oh. Me. Not much to tell. I said before, I grew up a little south and east of here. My dad was a teacher – well, is. Mom kept the home front in a semblance of organized. Wasn't easy. Two girls. Two boys. I always loved books – and organizing things. Ta Da! Librarian. Then, assistant director. It's a good job, and I like it. I know it doesn't sound exciting, but I feel secure in my routing, comfortable life. And, now that I think about it, I'm not sure I'd even want Lucy's job. Mine fits me perfectly." She looked up. Will was concentrating on her. Watching and listening. She had the feeling there was nothing in the world more important to him than her story. She found herself staring into those soft blue eyes and was quiet for too long. "Um, anyway, that's pretty much it." *Lame.*

"Nobody special?"

"Uh, no. After Robert and I split, I felt I just needed time." *Like fifty or sixty years. I'm giving up on the masculine gender. Even if . . .* Shannon's thoughts were interrupted by a buzzing in her purse.

"You need to get that?" he asked.

"I don't like to at dinner. It's the height of bad manners."

"You might want to check who it is – you know, just in case."

She reached into her purse and turned the phone so she could see the caller. Robert. "Well, speak of the devil," she said, as she hit 'decline.'

The rest of dinner was lovely, but uneventful. Will paid the check and escorted Shannon to her car.

"It was a lovely evening," she said smiling, "but you'd better have something to tell Lucy about what we reviewed."

"Simple, I'll tell her after our review I decided to have you send a condensed version of the information to me." He was smiling in return.

Shannon got into her car, started the engine, backed out of the space, and started down the road. Will watched the entire time.

"Oh, crap!" Shannon said out loud. *I've got to stop at the grocery store. Cookies for the office tomorrow.*

Shannon left the market with the cookies and pulled out onto the street. She was about a mile from home when she heard a pop. The front left corner of her car dropped. Careful not to use the brakes, she let the car coast to the curb. She stuck her head out the window and saw the left front tire was flat.

"Crap. Crap – crap – crap – crap – crap." She put the car in park and turned off the ignition. She felt as deflated as the tire. She checked the glove box for the owner's manual. It had been so long since she'd changed a tire, she had forgotten how.

As she stepped from the car, hoping the spare wasn't flat, flashing lights came on. Shannon shielded her eyes with her hand and saw it was a city police car.

"Evening, Ma'am. Looks like you've got some trouble."

"Yeah. On my way home. I hope the spare isn't flat, too. I don't know when it was checked last."

"You a member of the auto club?"

"Yes. Why?"

"Well, I'll give 'em a call and have them change it for you."

"Oh, thank you."

The city cop stayed until the auto club showed up – he said he was afraid the car – or she – might be hit. "People usually avoid hitting a cop car with the lights on – except for drunks. They seem to be drawn to the flashing lights – like moths," he said with a smile.

It only took about forty minutes for the auto club to get there and change the tire. Shannon thanked both the policeman and the man who'd changed her tire. It was past her bed time when she finally arrived home. With minimal pre-bed prep, she dropped into bed and off to sleep.

About the same time, Will arrived back at his hotel. His thoughts kept drifting to Shannon. What she might be doing. When he'd caught her falling, he'd also caught a whiff of her fragrance. Like her, it seemed to be soft – delicate – ethereal. He shook his head. He wouldn't get involved again. He might not be bad luck for women, but he didn't want to take the chance. He pulled off his outer garments, and dropped into bed.

Eight

Shortly after nine in the morning, Will walked in the door of Shannon's office, after knocking to request permission to enter. He was carrying his professional bag and a medium sized brown paper sack.

"You don't need to knock. If there isn't anyone here, just come in. If I'm in conference, I'll motion if it is important enough not to be interrupted."

"Thank you."

"What's in the bag?" Shannon took the proffered bag, opened it, and wide-eyed took out a coffee and cheese Danish. "Perfect. How'd you know?"

"I do investigative journalism as well as puff pieces."

"Sheri."

"Yup. Sheri. By the way, I had a lovely time last night. Better than it would have been otherwise. Thank you. And, yes, I owe you."

Blood rushed to her face. And, there was that bird again, in her stomach. She looked away and said, "Anything you might have owed me was paid up with that wonderful dinner. Thank you. I got cookies," she gestured to the table, "on the way home. Got a flat tire, too. Stopped at the store on the way home, then had a flat about a mile from my place. Policeman was there tout-de-suite. He stayed until the guy from the auto club arrived to change the tire. I dropped into bed when I finally got home."

"Flat tire?"

"Yeah. They're almost brand new, too. I'll have to check on the warranty. And, I'm driving around on that little thing they call a spare. I've never had much confidence in those. And, I've got meetings."

"I've got some time today. Why don't I take it and get it fixed? I'm sure you have plenty to do. It'll give me something to do before I have to call the office."

"I really hate to . . ."

"Don't' be silly. You're busy. I'd just be sitting twiddling my thumbs."

Shannon half closed one eye and cocked her head. "I'm not sure I've heard anyone say 'twiddling my thumbs,' much less actually do it in, oh, a couple of decades. Even then, it was my grandmother."

Will interlocked his fingers and started rotating his thumbs horizontally around each other. "See?"

Shannon rolled her eyes. "Fine. I *love* that car. Don't ding it. I'm sure you know where it is parked. Nobody absconded with my spot this morning." She gave a mock smile, but she was actually happy to be having this conversation. "Oh, you'll need my credit card."

"Now who's being silly. I'll let you know how much it is. Maybe you'll have to take me to dinner."

"Let me find out if Lucy has any marksmanship skills." Her phone rang. Her body sagged. She picked it up. "Hello? Yes, this is she. One moment." Shannon moved to get her purse out of a small closet. Will walked to meet her. As he did, they brushed. Shannon could swear that someone poured hot chocolate into her. A warm sweet feeling ran from head to toe, then settled in her stomach. She rummaged in her purse longer than she needed to, enjoying the warmth and having a bit of trouble focusing. She pulled out her keys and held them out to Will. As he reached to take them, she pulled back her hand and cocked her head. *Those blue eyes.*

Will smiled and mouthed, "I promise."

Nine

Will pulled out of the parking lot and headed through campus to the town's main drag, College Avenue. He didn't think it very original street name, especially for a place that was supposed to teach you to think. He headed toward town, what there was of it, on a sparsely congested, tree-lined, four-lane road. There were traffic lights every few blocks, and he doubted that the city had timed them for the traffic.

At the second light, Will noticed a dark blue sedan about four car-lengths back. Sole male occupant. He wasn't sure what made him suspicious. At the next corner, he turned right. The street was empty. He cruised slowly, as if looking for something. He looked in the rear-view mirror. Same car. Same distance. He took two lefts, then a right, putting him back on College. A minute later, the car was there again. Same distance back. Either somebody who doesn't know anything about tailing someone, or someone out to make a statement.

He pulled in to a tire store he had Googled earlier. He sat in the car until the dark blue car passed. He hadn't seen Robert the day before, but he had a good idea this was Robert.

An employee approached the car. "Howdy. Looks like you'll be needing a new tire."

"Uh, yes. A friend's car. She had a flat last night. I was wondering if you could take a look at it."

"Sure. No problem. Fix it if possible. Isn't always."

"Do you mind if I watch?"

"Well, not supposed to. Insurance and all. Nobody supposed to be in the bays but the employees."

Will handed him fifty dollars. "Just want to see what might have caused the damage."

"Okay." The employee, Fred, if you believed the name badge on his shirt, had Will pull the car into a bay.

Will opened the trunk and pulled out the damaged tire. Fred rolled it to the swing arm. The tire was already flat, so it was a simple task to remove the first side of the tire.

"Before you pull off the second side, can I look to see if there is any debris?"

"Okay."

Will first looked in the tire, then ran his hand carefully around the inside. He found what felt like a small pebble and pulled it out. He dumped it into his other palm and looked at it in the light.

"A rock?" asked Fred.

"No. Not a rock. Bullet. Probably a .22." Will was not happy. The implications of a .22 caliber bullet in Shannon's tire and an obsessive, possessive ex-boyfriend who didn't think he was an ex-boyfriend weren't good.

"That's a rare shot," said Fred. "What are the odds of somebody accidentally hitting a tire?"

"Yeah," said Will absentmindedly. Then, "Do you sell run flats here? Something that looks like the tires that are already on the car?"

"Sure, but I'm not sure you should have a run flat on one side and these others on the other wheels. Might make the car unstable. Especially at speed. This one can't be fixed, hole punched in the side wall. I've got this exact tire. Can have it done in fifteen minutes."

"Thanks, uh, Fred, but I'd like to get the run flats. Four. All around. What the heck. A spare, as well."

"Need a new wheel. Not going to be cheap. Must be a special friend."

"Yeah. She is." Will wondered why he was doing all this. But he knew. A protective instinct. He might not be here for long, but he'd do what he could. He'd be gone in a day or two. Folks would have to sort out their own problems. But there was something about Shannon. Something beautiful and innocent. He knew. It was Ariel. Penance. When he thought about Shannon, there was a happy glow inside him. He liked that feeling and he didn't like the idea of her being stalked or hurt.

Fred was done in an hour. Will paid him and gave him an extra hundred dollars for the quick service. Fred actually tried to turn the hundred down, saying that the set of run flats and wheel had made his day.

Will drove back to campus, hypervigilant for anyone following him. Apparently, if it was Robert, he was happy to see he'd made Shannon spend time and money on the repair. Will parked in Shannon's spot and walked back to her office.

Shannon was busy looking at a financial printout when Will entered the room. She looked up when he entered. "So, what do I owe you? Was it hard to fix?"

"Uh, no. Really cheap as a matter of fact. I've got the receipt . . ." Will started digging through his pockets, feigning to look for the receipt. "I must have dropped it."

"Please. That is SO lame. Did that even work in high school?"

"Hey! I'll have you know it worked GREAT in high school. Got me three dates with Marci Hightower. Cheerleader and everything."

"Fine. I'll buy you dinner. Not a date. Dinner." *It's a date!*

"You say that now." *It's a date!*

Lunch was delivered. Will called his office.

"Bad news, I'm afraid," he said as he left the small storage room and entered Shannon's office.

"What?"

"I was talking with my editor and he thought getting more information on this motorcycle jump gone bad might make a reasonable story. He said he'd like to have me stick around a couple of days and get some more information to see if it pans out."

"Uh huh. And he just happened to hear about it how? Not sure it made the papers in – where is your editor?"

"I may have mentioned it. Seems odd. Sometimes, 'seems odd' turn out to be the best stories."

"Uh huh. Not just sticking around so you can woo Lucy, are

you?" Shannon was barely holding her laugh.

"Yeah. That's it. You found me out." Now, they were both laughing.

Ten

Robert Barr sat in the semi-darkened light of his apartment. On the coffee table in front of him sat four empty beer cans and two cold slices of pizza in an open box. A beer can half-filled with warming, flat beer was in his hand. His feet covered the area of the coffee table not occupied by the pizza and empty cans.

He'd turned the television to his favorite channel – one featuring all outdoor shows. The sound was low. The current show was about hunting bears in the wild.

Yeah, that's the way it should be. The big and strong ones take the females they want. The females don't go sayin', 'This isn't working out for me. I want something else, and I'm leaving.'

Robert squeezed the can until it started to crush. Remembering it still contained beer, he stopped crushing it and finished off the contents. There was a commercial break. After five beers, he lifted his feet from the coffee table, stood, and headed for the toilet. A scented candle on the back of the toilet was the last reminder that Shannon used to come here. He didn't particularly like it – "No need for all that girlie stuff in my place," but he left it there to remind him of her. *She'll appreciate that I kept it when she comes back,* he reasoned.

Robert returned to the living room. The walls were bare. She didn't like that. He thought about putting up a few pictures. If he did, they'd be his choice. *Can't have a woman decorating your place. Even if – when – she moves in, it's to take care of what's mine, not to pretend it's all hers.*

Still, he missed having her around. Having her showed the guys that he could get a woman. He'd get mad when she didn't want to do some of the things he wanted to do. That was her place.

The show went to another commercial. A guy hunting in the woods. He thought back to last night. He'd been able to shoot her tire. *Took three shots, but the rifle is semi-auto, so that doesn't matter. Movin' car, and all. When the cop showed up, it really pissed me off. I coulda slid right up behind her, changed that tire, and she'd a* been grateful. Except for the cop. Might have asked about the gun, too. Then, the cop stands around until the auto club guy gets there and changes her tire.

He popped the sixth beer and took a healthy swig. *Then, there's that new guy. I'm going to have to deal with him. Just who the hell . . . Do my heart good to shoot him.* He closed his eyes and pictured shooting Will Daniels three or four times before walking up to him lying on the ground, spitting on him, then shooting him in the head. *Nice thing about a .22. You can shoot something over and over before it dies. Let it suffer. No. Not yet. Much as it feels nice to think about it, I can't really do that right now.*

He picked up a piece of cold pizza, folded it in half the long way and began stuffing it into his mouth.

I'm going to have to find some way to let Shannon know that if she were still with me, that flat tire woulda been no big thing. I woulda gotten there, fixed it, and then she'd a been grateful. Grateful enough . . .

Eleven

"Okay. So why is your editor interested in a ten-year-old story about a failed motorcycle jump?" Shannon's tone was mildly prosecutorial.

"It's just odd."

"How?"

"It's not like jumps like this are done every day, but this is a big jump. Especially for a first try. But anybody trying to try it can get the parameters. Evel Knievel made very similar jumps successfully. You need a ramp at a certain angle and a specific launch speed."

"Well, maybe they didn't get it right."

"If it were your life, wouldn't you double check everything? Especially since it had been done before."

"Well, duh! But I wouldn't be doing it anyway."

"So, could you see what the ramp angle and speed would be – just as a little favor?"

Shannon gave him a quizzical look, shrugged her shoulders, and turned to her computer. In a few minutes, she said, "According to successful jumps by Mr. Knievel, for a jump that long, assuming the weight of the motorcycle and rider of about 500 pounds, the ramp should be between nineteen and twenty-three degrees and the take-off speed should be 80 miles per hour."

"Are you sure?"

"Of course, I'm sure. I double checked it."

"Okay. I already knew the parameters."

"Then why..."

"You aren't even going to make the jump and you double checked it. There should be no way they missed by that much."

"Okay. They messed up. But the guy was lucky. He was hurt, but not even too badly. Even the doctors said it was a miracle."

"But he would have hit the rocks at about 75 miles per hour.

75! Not in a car, which would have been bad enough, but on a motorcycle – with handlebars, gas tank, and the frame."

"But he didn't get hurt - well too badly. I mean it can happen."

"I don't happen to believe in miracles. My dad used to take me to magic shows."

"You like magic?"

"No. The point is, he used to tell me there is no magic. It's all illusion. He'd take me so we could figure out how the tricks were done. It stuck with me. Whenever there's a miracle, I see it as an illusion and I want to know how it was done."

"Wow! Christmas and Easter must have been real downers at your house."

Will gave her a faux withering look. "The holidays were fine, thank you. Maybe I can make you a bit of a believer."

"Or disbeliever?"

"What's your mobile number?"

"Why?" Quickly she added, "not that I mind."

"I want to set something up. I'll call when I'm ready."

"Sounds mysterious," she said as she gave him her cell number on a piece of paper.

Will entered the number into his phone, then took the paper, stuffed it into his mouth and began chewing.

"What the ..."

"Jush kippen it seckrit," he mumbled.

Shannon was laughing so hard she missed him dropping the paper into his hand and then into the trash can beside her desk.

*   *   *   *   *   *   *   *   *   *   *

"Then, what happened?" asked Sheri

Shannon told her.

Sheri laughed as she said, "Sounds like a nice guy. And a hunk, from what I've seen."

"He's a hunk, alright. Thanks to you telling him about my fondness for cheese Danish, I'm going to end up a chunk – to his hunk."

"Huh. A chunk and a hunk in a bunk. Sounds like you're interested."

"What? No. He's only been here a couple of days. His life is so hectic. There's no routine to it. Anyway, I'm trying to figure out what he is 'setting up,' obviously for my benefit."

"A special thing AND a dinner. Sounding like a date to me."

"It's not a date.

"Even you don't sound convinced."

"It would be nice to have a date. But this is business – sort of – you know."

"That's even less convincing."

"I don't know anything about him. I live and work here, and I like my quiet, routine. He – I don't even know where he lives or works – except he travels a lot. I mean, how would that work? Not that I'm really wondering how it would work."

"For somebody who isn't interested, and who is insisting this isn't a date, the train seems to be a fair distance down the tracks."

"I'm not even sure what that means. I just . . ." Shannon's mobile phone rang. "What? Where? I . . . Okay." Then to Sheri, "I guess whatever it is got worked out. He wants me to meet him in the back of the library."

"Well," said Sheri with a sly grin, "let's hope it is an early dinner then a trip to a little quaint bed and breakfast where . . ." Shannon slammed the door behind her to cut off Sheri's fun.

Twelve

Shannon navigated the hallways to the back of the building. *Sure, he's a hunk. Better than I've seen around here in ages, but our worlds are different. How would we even . . . Why am I even thinking about this?* She shook her head to clear the thoughts.

She left the building. Will was standing beside the rented SUV.

"I hope it's okay, but I want to demonstrate why I think the motorcycle accident is, at the very least, odd. I hope you're game for some fun."

"And my part in this would be?"

"Just sit and watch. Sit and watch." He said it with a smile.

Will walked around the vehicle and opened the passenger side door for her. He waited for her to enter then closed the door before walking back to the driver's side.

Shannon was feeling secretly pleased at the gesture. Will walked around the front of the SUV.

They drove about ten minutes and arrived at a motorcycle dealership. A number of men and women were standing near what were apparently their motorcycles. All were wearing leather jackets with FCMC emblazoned on the back.

"So . . ." started Shannon.

"Ever ride a motorcycle?"

"What? Wait! I thought . . ."

"I said sit and watch. I didn't say where you would be sitting. You'll be safe."

"I – I don't know. How will I be safe? Are you going to drive?"

They left the SUV, Will more quickly than Shannon. Again, he opened her door and held it for her. A good-looking stocky man, maybe in his forties, with a tan and somewhat weathered face walked up and held out his hand. "Good afternoon. My name is Jack. Jack Hawkins."

"I called around. Mr. Hawkins . . ."

"Jack, please."

"Jack," Will started again, "is the president of this motorcycle club. He also happens to be a police officer who rides motorcycles in his work. Never had an accident."

"Jack arranged for us to go for a ride this afternoon," continued Will.

"I – I – I . . ." started Shannon.

"So, your friend . . ." started Jack.

"I'm beginning to have doubts about him being a friend," said Shannon. She noticed her hands and legs were wobbly and that bird in her stomach was acting up again.

"You'll be fine," continued Jack. "Your – uh, alleged – friend has convinced me he can ride, and after talking with him, I thought we'd take a one together."

"I – I'm not sure . . ."

A pretty blond was handing Shannon a helmet and jacket. "Got to look the part, Sweetie. They're magical. They'll keep you safe. If they even got scratched, Jack wouldn't want to face the consequences." The other women and some of the men laughed. Somebody said, "You tell her, Brittany."

Shannon wasn't sure they'd fit. Unfortunately, they did.

Jack was talking. Shannon was listening - sort of. Will was sliding into a jacket and picked up a helmet.

"Why no seat belt?"

"That's a very good question, Shannon. In a car, you are inside a safety cage. The belt keeps you in your seat and makes sure you don't get bounced around off the sides of the cage. If you had an accident on a motorcycle, you would be between the motorcycle and whatever it impacted."

Shannon thought that 'impacted' was a euphemism for what really happened, but she kept her thoughts to herself. She noticed her hands and her legs felt weak.

"So, we wear protective gear around ourselves. And we ride safely. See? No scratches or tears." He said it with a smile, but she was thinking, *this could all be new gear, just to fool me.*

"Ready?"

Will slid onto one of the bikes. The motorcycle rumbled to life. Shannon found herself climbing onto the motorcycle behind Will, hoping he actually knew how to ride a bike.

Shannon thought she might want to be sick, but there was nothing there. She was almost happy for the shaking of the machine. She could no longer separate the shakes that belonged to her.

He turned his head and asked, "Okay?"

Shannon nodded indicating 'Yes,' but she didn't understand why she was responding opposite to what she felt.

There was a slight bump as Jack put the machine in gear. Shannon wrapped her arms tightly around Will's waist and pulled herself tightly against him. The motorcycle started of slowly, moving in a straight line. Shannon felt the breeze and the smoothness of the ride. She started to relax just a bit. Well, not that much.

Will drove back and forth slowly, then a bit faster. He made some slow turns and figure eights. He picked up speed – a bit. Then, he stopped. He turned and asked, "Doing okay?" She nodded.

Thirteen

Shannon sat at her desk. One bite was missing from a personal sized cheese and mushroom pizza on her desk.

"So, I see you worked up quite an appetite on your adventure. Care to tell me about it?" Sheri had come into her office and sat in one of two upholstered armchairs facing the desk at an angle.

"I don't know what I'm feeling. It was all a mixture of terrifying, then exciting. But my brain and my mouth are clearly not in sync."

"How so?"

"He said he wanted to demonstrate why it seemed odd to him that the guy who missed the motorcycle jump should have died or at the very least had extremely serious injuries. He said we were going to have a ride on a motorcycle. My brain was telling me to say 'no way,' but all I did was look at him. Then, when he opened my door ..."

"He opens car doors?"

"Right. *That's* the important takeaway from this conversation. Anyway, when he opened my door, I was going to tell him there was no way he was getting me on a motorcycle."

"Did you?"

"No. Like an idiot, I got out of the car. There was a group of four, yes, four I think, motorcycles and maybe six or seven people. He introduced me to a guy named Jack. Forties. Tan. A bit weathered."

"Ooooo. Two hunks."

"Shush. Jack is a motorcycle cop.

"Sounds like ..."

"And married. Anyway, Jack said we'd go for a ride as a group. Somehow, Will wangled a Harley Davidson Electra Glide Classic."

"Wow! Nice bike!"

"You know motorcycles?"

"A little. I read. Enough to know this is a cushy bike, not some little crotch rocket."

"A little what? Anyway, I ended up behind him – and the whole time my brain is going No! No! No! There was no seat belt, and I asked why. When I got the answer, I started picturing myself strapped in a hospital bed, sucking nutrition out of a tube for the rest of my life. Then, Will started the motorcycle, and I could feel it rumbling between my legs."

"Okay, we're getting to an interesting part here."

Shannon gave Sheri a withering look. It didn't help.

"He asked me if I was ready. Again, my brain said No! and I nodded yes. There's some kind of disconnect there. So, he started slowly. I was wrapped so tightly around him I'm not sure he could breathe."

"Again. Bike vibrating between your legs and you're wrapped around a hunk."

"Really?" But despite her seeming shock, she was reliving the feeling of being wrapped around him, pulled against his hips with her thighs, his body against her and the vibrating machine. Suddenly, there was heat throughout her body, but centered deep within her abdomen. Her face reddened. She looked away from Sheri to avoid her eyes.

"Just saying. Hey, you okay?"

Shannon was finally able to control herself. "He did some slow back and forth, some turns, and some figure eights. After a few minutes, we headed out on the road and ended up riding up Poudre Canyon. I'll have to admit, the feeling of the wind, and being out in the elements, it was kind of exciting. He kept asking if I was okay. We passed by the canyon edge close enough that I would have hated hitting the rocks, and we were only doing about 45 – he said later. We came back and I got off the bike, I wasn't sure I hadn't wet myself."

"Good wet or bad wet?"

"Sheri!" but sitting there now, she wasn't' sure.

"Well, from what I've heard so far, it sounds like a combination of the worst car wreck I've ever been in and the best sex I've ever had. Not that the sex was mind-blowing, but you get the idea. I just wanted to know which won out."

"Even if I knew, I wouldn't tell you. But I could learn to enjoy it."

"So, what did Will say?"

"We were pretty much quiet on the way back. He said he wanted to give me time to process it all. But he's right, that crash would have been devastating. A week or two in the hospital wouldn't even have been a good start. So, I guess he's convinced me. Whether it rates investigation, well that's another thing."

"Oh, speaking of Will and investigations, he got a call while you guys were gone. I got it on your phone. Some woman named Clode."

"Clode?"

"Yeah, but she had a French accent, so who knows what it really is. I asked for her last name and she got a bit uppity. She said, 'Tell Will – she said it Weel – that Clode called and wants him to call back. Clode Vee Yay, but he will know from Clode. He has my number.'"

"Wow. Weird. I wonder if . . . Oh crap! Vee Yay? Oh crap!"

"What?"

"There was a French model Claudine Viller – pronounced Vee Yay. She burned up the runways for about five years and left at the top of her game because she said she had a brain and walking up and down showing off clothes was mind numbing. She left modeling and now she's doing god knows what. And, she's a friend of Will'?"

"For someone who isn't sure she's interested . . ."

"Shush. Maybe I am. Maybe I'm not. My brain tells me maybe I'm not, but my brain has been pretty much useless lately. If whatever is left is telling me I'm interested, I'd rather not have to battle Claudine Viller. Crap."

"Maybe she isn't his type."

"Oh, right. I can see why guys wouldn't be interested in a tall, gorgeous, long-legged model who makes your mouth drop open. Oh, and this one can apparently think. Crap. Well, maybe you're right. Maybe he likes shorter, chubbier, pasty-white ones with spots. God! I sound like I'm describing an English spaniel."

"Wow! Somebody needs to work on their self-image."

"I know exactly what I look like."

"Did your annual review, did you? Anyway, there was a show on years ago – Gilligan's Island. There were two women, Ginger, a movie star, and Mary Ann, a girl next door. When male viewers were polled, 96 percent would have wanted to be with Mary Ann, not Ginger."

"Yes, I did my annual inventory. And, your study shows that I would be most popular with prepubescent males. By the way, Ginger was a red head." Shannon said it while holding her red hair out.

Fourteen

Shannon and Sheri sat in Shannon's office. Shannon was mildly upset with her friend who had surreptitiously punched in to listen to Will who was calling his office from Sheri's.

"Bonjour. Claudine Viller."

"Bonjour Claudine. C'est William a l'appareil."

"William. Why don't you call me?"

"I'm calling you now."

"No. I mean to just talk."

"I'm working. I'm on assignment. I've been doing things."

"On a ten-year-old motorcycle accident. That's not a story. It is an alibi. I miss you and want to talk to you."

"Claudine, we've talked about this before. We work together. It won't be any more than that."

"Is this because of her? The woman in your past? Or, is it because there is another woman? I know there is."

"It's America." His tone was dark. "There are a lot of women."

"You know what I mean. I mean one special woman. You are having an affair, no?"

"No. I'm not having an affair." Suddenly, he was drained.

"But there is a woman. Women know these things. Tell me. Is she pretty?"

Will seemed lost in thought. He looked up and across the hallway.

"This woman," Claudine continued, "does she remind you of her? Cheveux roux, peut etre?"

Shannon didn't dare look up from the desk. She didn't want to give them away. Sheri was facing away from her office, leaned forward and said, "I don't remember a lot of my French, but 'cheveux roux,' is red hair." Shannon's heart was pounding so hard she thought people in the hallway would hear it, and she knew from the heat she felt that her face had turned a bright red.

"I'm working on a story," he said quietly, unconvincingly.

"I did not hear. What did you say?" asked Claudine.

"Nothing."

"I could make you happy."

"You could make a lot of men happy. And they could make you happy. I don't fall into that group of men."

"I know you just need time to realize."

They heard Will sigh. "Look. I'll be here another two weeks, probably. I'll let the boss know when I done. Good luck Claudine. Au revoir."

"Deux semaine, oui. Je surais ici. Au revoir."

They waited until both Claudine and Will had disconnected, then disconnected Shannon's phone. "Holy crap! Rack another one up for Mary Ann."

Shannon got up from her desk and hurried to her office door. Heat burned deep within her and there was a tingling. Her face was hot. Her heart hammered in her chest. "I've got to get to the ladies' room and hide for a little bit – calm down. Oh, my god." *What am I feeling? What am I supposed to feel?*

Fifteen minutes later, Shannon returned, somewhat composed. Sheri was seated in one of the armchairs. Will was seated in the other. Shannon gave him a 'hello' as carefully as she could. She didn't dare look at him. Her heart had settled in the ladies' room, but it started up again when she saw Will in her office. She was settling down again, pretending to check her e-mail, when she saw an e-mail from Lucy.

"Crap!"

"What?" said Sheri and Will almost in unison.

"Lucy. She says she needs donor numbers – the whole shebang – tomorrow morning for a meeting."

"I don't remember anything about a meeting," said Sheri. "Wait a minute. You don't suppose ..."

They both looked at Will.

"You didn't happen to mention a dinner with Shannon tonight, did you?"

"I don't remember. I might have. Why?"

"Looks like Lucy is trying to ruin Shannon's evening."

"You're kidding. Really?"

"God, even if it goes well, it will take me until ten o'clock to get all that stuff together," said Shannon.

"Can I help?" asked Will.

"No. This is all mine," Shannon was crestfallen.

"I'll help," said Sheri.

"You better not let Lucy know, or we'll both be off to the gallows."

"Is it really that bad?" asked Will.

"Yes. She can be a, uh, . . ."

"Got it. Okay. Let me check a couple of things out. Let me know when you think you'll be done. Then, text me when you are. I think I can come up with a decent dinner arrangement."

"At ten o'clock at night?"

Fifteen

At 9:45, Shannon sent the text. She met Will at the library entrance.

"So. Were you able to come up with anything in our sleepy little town?"

"I think so."

He walked her to his vehicle and held her door.

"You know, in this day and age, women don't expect to have doors held for them," she said. "We're capable."

"True. In this case, it shows respect. And deference."

Shannon's face warmed, and she looked away, in spite of herself.

The drive was less than ten minutes – to an older part of the city. He parked and took her by the hand, leading her down a relatively dark alley.

"Uh …"

"Don't worry. I have it on good authority this place is worth it."

Halfway down the alley, he turned toward an entrance which was down a few steps from the alley level. There was a dark green door, lit only by a dim bulb. After stepping down a few steps, Shannon saw under the light, there was a painting of what looked like a red lady's garter.

Will knocked three times. A peep hole opened and he said, "Joe sent me."

Shannon rolled her eyes, but the peephole closed and the door opened.

Shannon stepped into the space as a man dressed in a tuxedo said, "Evening folks. Welcome to the Red Garter."

The room was small, maybe 800 square feet. The walls were red brick – old. The floor was covered in what looked like a Persian rug. The ceiling was painted tin. The décor was Art Deco. Smooth jazz played quietly. There were five or six couples at tables. They were shown to a corner booth, room for just two.

"Where did you," started Shannon.

"My job. I love it and I'm very good at it. When we do travel pieces, I get to know the natives. They tell me about their lives, about where and how they live. They also share secret places they love. I don't usually write about those. They stay secret."

"You've only been here a couple of days. That couldn't be enough time."

Will looked around. "Finding places like this is the reason I'd never give up my work."

The waiter appeared and presented menus with limited selections. Both opted for the Niçoise salad with seared tuna. And a glass of pinot blanc.

"So, never going to give up your work?" Shannon felt a touch of sadness and hollowness as she asked.

Will set his wine glass down. "Well, nobody can see what will happen in the future, but I can't imagine sitting in an office wearing a tie, shuffling papers and futzing with budgets." After a pause, "I didn't mean . . ."

"No. I get it. Okay for the rest of us, but a death sentence for you."

"I didn't mean it that way. You love being a librarian – the library. Without you, there wouldn't be libraries. The whole world would be stupider than it is. Hard to believe that would be possible. I'm very happy there are people like you who love that work. I love the freedom I have with my work. Hey! It got me here, someplace I might never have gotten to otherwise. And, I got to meet you – well, after a quick ice bath."

Shannon laughed in spite of herself.

The salads arrived.

"So, don't you want to work at the library as long as you can?"

"I like my work, and I do think it is important, but it doesn't provide life meaning for me. I'm satisfied, but I think there is something more than work."

"Family?"

"Mine, or do I want one? A family might be nice, but after Robert – well, I've kind of given up."

"Robert doesn't represent the totality of male gender."

"Maybe, but my experience so far hasn't led me to believe my prince is waiting for me out there."

"I'm sorry. I seem to have gotten us on a thread that I shouldn't have."

"No, it's okay. It is what it is."

"I noticed you have a nice collection of travel books in your office. Interested in travel?"

"The books allow me to go to many different places – without leaving here. If I've got fifteen minutes, I can visit Rome or Cairo."

"Wouldn't you like to experience them first-hand?"

"I can see what I want. I don't have to get lost in a foreign city, eat things that will make me sick, or sleep in a run-down hotel. Not to mention the time spent getting there and the money, well, the money spent. I know it doesn't seem adventurous to you, but I visit places and keep my routine. My routine is comfortable and important to me."

They finished their salads and opted to split an order of tiramisu. They ate in silence.

"We should probably go," said Will, gesturing for the waiter.

"No. I'm actually feeling good. Could we stay for just a bit?"

"Yes, sir?"

Shannon said, "Nothing for me."

"Lagavulin, please, and the check."

The waiter returned with the drink and a folder. Will took a quick look and placed cash in the folder.

Shannon leaned against Will, "May I?"

"Certainly." And he placed his arm around her. His closeness produced a warm satisfaction that wrapped her.

The food, wine, quiet soothing music, and the warmth of Will close to her made her close her eyes. She was surprised it was almost an hour later when she opened them. "Oh! I'm sorry," she said starting to straighten up.

"You're fine. They aren't ready to boot us out."

"Did I?"

"Did you what? You didn't snore, drool, or say anything rude. You were a perfect lady."

"I doubt that, but thank you – especially if you're lying."

Will escorted her to the door and out. He thanked the maître d'.

"Thank you for a lovely evening. I enjoyed myself very much. I'm still amazed that you found this place."

They returned to the SUV and he drove her home.

He parked in the drive and walked her to the door. They paused, then without saying anything, he put his arms around her waist and pulled her to him. Their eyes met, then their lips touched. Softly. She felt a warm feeling pour through her. When it moved through her core, it heated and smoldered. The kiss ended. Their lips parted. Their eyes met again. Shannon's arms were around his neck and she moved to him, this time crushing her lips against his. They moved together until their stomachs touched. The heat exploded. Her hand ran down his back, stopping at his waist and pulling him in. Their breathing was hard and fast. Her heart was pounding in her chest.

A rock shattered one of Shannon's windows. Shannon jumped.

Sixteen

Will turned to search for the assailant. As he turned, used his right hand to move her behind his back. Dark bushes were all he could see around the perimeter.

"You're not staying here tonight."

"But . . ."

"They'll have an extra room at the hotel. We can deal with this in the morning."

Shannon was terrified, but she drew a measure of comfort from Will saying 'We can deal with this in the morning,' instead of 'You can deal with this in the morning.'

They drove to Will's hotel and he got Shannon a room on his floor, across the hall. When they got to the room, Shannon said, "Could I just stay with you? I really don't want to be alone right now, no matter how safe it really is."

"Sure."

They went into his room. He got her a set of pajamas. They were almost big enough for her to swim in. She opted for one of his t-shirts instead of the top that kept revealing more of her than she was comfortable showing. Will put on a pair of running shorts and t-shirt. He started to head for the couch.

"No. Please. I need you close."

So, he came to bed and put his arms around her. He felt her relax almost immediately.

Seventeen

Shannon opened her eyes slowly. She didn't want the night to end. She thought about how nice it might be to do this for the rest of her life. A bit of dawn was coming through the light-blocking hotel curtains. She moved and didn't feel Will beside her. She turned to find him gone. Her eye caught the display on the clock radio – 8:07. *Rats! I've got to get up and get to work. I hadn't thought ahead to get work clothes. And if I show up in what I was wearing last night . . . No. Even if Lucy doesn't notice, Sheri will be unbearable.* Her thoughts were interrupted by a key clicking the lock in the door.

"Oh, good morning Sunshine. I thought I'd let you sleep as long as possible." Will stood in the doorway, a bag and garment bag in hand.

"God! I've got to get ready for work. And, I forgot to pick up anything to wear."

"I went to the hotel store. I found you some things that might work for you. I checked the sizes in your things – I hope you don't mind. Anyway, it will keep you from doing the walk of shame. I know Sheri wouldn't let it go."

"You seem to know Sheri pretty well. How do you know about the walk of shame?"

"Guys have the same thing, although – you know guys – it's more like a celebration than actual walk of shame. We get high fives. Here," he said handing her the bags, "I can leave so you can try them on."

"I can do it in the – um – powder room. No need for you to leave. Especially after all you've done."

Shannon headed for the bath. She showered and dried off. Then, she opened the bags. Inside the handled bag were pushup bra and matching briefs. They looked high-end. Shannon blushed. She wasn't sure whether she should have a man buying her lingerie and blushed a bit more when she thought about him seeing her, knowing she was wearing what he had picked out. She slid them on. They fit perfectly. The garment bag held a pair of black fitted formal yoga pants. She wondered if she could squeeze into them. Also, in the bag was an oyster silk blouse. First, she pulled on the yoga pants. They were just a bit tight, especially around her derriere. Everywhere else, they were perfect. *Maybe*, she thought, *I just don't show off my bottom.* The silk blouse felt heavenly, soft and smooth against her skin. The only problem was it had a bit more décolletage than she was used to. Or was it a bit less. Anyway, it was somewhat daring. She left the blouse untucked if only to cover at least some of her bottom. She would have preferred it to go to her knees, but then . . . Shannon headed for the main room.

"So, I was thinking," Will started. When Shannon entered the room, he stopped and said, "Wow! And by Wow, I mean that I don't think Wow is enough."

"Well, YOU bought them," she said, deciding to give a little twirl. "And just how do you know how to buy women's clothes Mr. There's Nobody in my Life?"

"I know a woman who shares fashion ideas."

"And the, um, undergarments?"

"Woman in the store helped me. Oh, by the way, I got shoes and these."

Shannon opened a small box to find diamond stud earrings and a pear-shaped diamond pendant on a white gold chain. She gasped.

"Don't panic. They're cubic zirconia."

"No. You can't. This cost . . . I don't know, but it all cost too much. Really."

"I'll hide it in my expense account. I've got a lot of latitude. I may have to mention you in the story. You know, just to keep it on the up and up."

"And your boss won't question why you are buying," she used her hand to indicate everything.

"You'd be surprised. My boss, recluse that he is, is also a hopeless romantic. He picks his people well, and he wants them to have somewhat of a free rein. This purchase will get a smile. Oh, don't forget the shoes."

Another bag contained a pair of suede block-heel pumps. "No. Really. I can't . . ."

"Sure you can. Because there isn't anything tied to them. Now . . ." There was a knock on the door.

"Room service."

Will walked to the door and opened it. A waiter pushed in a cart. There was coffee and juice and two covered plates. Will tipped the waiter, who removed the covers from the plates, revealing scrambled eggs, bacon, toast, and on one, a cheese Danish.

Shannon went to the bathroom and returned wearing a t-shirt. "Not taking a chance with the silk blouse." She kissed Will on the cheek, then, they devoured the breakfast.

"I'll drop you at work. You can call the police and arrange a time for them to meet you at your place to file a report. You've got to, you know."

"Yes, I know."

Eighteen

Shannon walked into her office a few minutes after nine. Technically, she was late, but Lucy wasn't going to say anything, especially after keeping her late the night before. *God! Was that just last night. So much happened.* She closed her eyes and recreated that warm and comforting feeling.

The door opened behind her. It was Sheri.

"So, I came to find out – Holy Shit!"

"What?!"

"You. That ...! Man, you look hot. Just the right amount of great fashion with just a touch of ... uh. I've never seen that outfit before, but if this is the new you, I really want to find out what got into you – if you catch my drift."

"Sheri! It wasn't like that. It was nice. Very nice. And we were both clothed."

"I notice you didn't say 'fully' clothed."

"Why are you doing this?"

"Because my best friend in the world went out on a mysterious date – by the way, you'll have to fill me in on the where you went – and today she looks stunning – and very satisfied."

"We didn't have sex. There."

"Boo!"

"It WAS a wonderful night. Well, mostly wonderful. But even the not-so-wonderful parts led to wonderful things."

"Okay. I'm all ears. I want all the details. Mostly, I want the lurid details, but you can sprinkle those."

Shannon told her about the after-hours club she'd never known about before. She talked about how great it was to cuddle with Will while they sat in their own cozy booth. She hated for the night to end and just when it almost did, a rock smashed her window, and Will had taken her to his hotel.

"I think I'm going to have to do something about Robert," said Shannon.

"So," said Sheri with a smile, "you don't think it was Lucy?"

"Lucy?"

"Yeah. Maybe she found out you two had dinner and was mad."

"Really? No. That would get her arrested and fired. Besides, she doesn't stay up that late. No. It was Robert. Creepy him staking my place out."

"Creepy doesn't even start to describe it. So, you went to his hotel. Hopefully, they didn't have an extra room."

"So, we went to his hotel. They had an extra room," said Shannon. Sheri deflated. "But when we got to the room, I said I was just too scared and wanted to stay with him."

Sheri brightened. "Way to go girl. Don't give up."

Shannon gave her a look you would give to a five-year-old when you disapproved of her behavior. "It wasn't that way. After the rock, I was really scared and wasn't going to feel safe by myself."

"Whatever you have to tell yourself. Works for me."

"I'm telling you it wasn't – well, okay, maybe a small part. He gave me a set of pj's. The top was WAY too big. So, I stole one of his t-shirts."

"The top would have gotten you farther."

"Stop!"

"He was going to sleep on the couch, but I asked him to hold me. And that's the way we spent the night. Until this morning when I woke and he was gone – getting me this outfit. What do you think? Slacks too tight – in the – um – back?"

"God No! Those are perfect. Tighter than you usually wear, but they really show off your – dare I say cute – behind."

"Cute I'm not. Well, not there anyway. At least I wasn't stupid enough to ask if he got his fashion sense from Clode."

"But, god, Shannon. You really look great in that outfit. I said it before, chalk another one up for Mary Ann, baby." Both women laughed.

Lucy entered the office, and both women stopped laughing. "Shannon, I'm ..." Lucy stopped in mid-sentence, looking at Shannon from head to toe. "I haven't seen you wear that before."

"It's new. I thought I'd wear it to the office, I don't get out much."

"Very nice." Lucy said it slowly and almost as if she didn't know she was saying it. "Anyway, I just wanted to stop by and thank you for your work last night. It helped a lot. I hope it didn't spoil any plans you might have had."

"Um, no. Things seemed to work out okay. Thank you."

Lucy turned and left, a somewhat puzzled look on her face.

"I'd say things worked out very well indeed," said Sheri.

Nineteen

Shannon checked e-mails and voice mail. There were only two items that needed a quick response, although she thought, *It's not like the world will come to an end if I let these sit. People think the smallest things are SO important.*

She called the police department and arranged to meet with an officer at 10 AM, then she stopped by Lucy's office. Lucy's assistant made a big show of looking at Lucy's schedule to see if Lucy had a moment. Fed up, Shannon said, "Just tell her I have to meet the police at my place to file a report."

Lucy's assistant's mouth dropped open, "Wha...?"

But Shannon had already turned and was walking away, a smile on her face. *Serves her right for being such a self-centered witch.*

Shannon walked to her car then drove to her place. She parked in the drive but decided not to enter the home. She didn't want to disturb anything the police might want to see. The officer arrived a few minutes later. The patrol car parked on the street. Officer Dwight Fredericks was an impressive looking man. Six feet tall and muscular, he was big even without the vest.

"Mornin', Ma'am. Dwight Fredericks, Fort Collins PD. I understand you had some vandalism here last night you wish to report?"

"Uh, yes, officer. I was coming home late from a dinner and before I could get in the door, someone threw a rock through my window – there," she said pointing to the shattered window.

"Could it have been a rock thrown out of a tire?"

"I don't think so. I didn't hear any vehicles. It scared me, so I spent the night in a hotel. I haven't been in the house since it happened. I thought you might want to see it before I went in."

"Well, we'll take a look."

They went to the front door. Officer Fredericks looked at the window, took a few photographs, and wrote some notes in his notebook.

Shannon opened the door. Officer Fredericks followed her into the entry. To the left, on the living room rug was a rock the size of a baseball and shards of glass.

"Well, doesn't look like this could have been thrown out of a tire – least not any I've seen around here. Wait here, please. I'd like to check the house. Clear it."

Shannon stood in the entry while Officer Fredericks went from room to room, making sure there wasn't anyone else in the home.

"Appears to be secure, Ma'am. Back door locked. Windows as well. Nobody hiding in any rooms or closets." He took photographs of the window from the inside as well as of the rock and debris. He made some measurements and wrote in his notebook. He picked up the rock. "Never get any prints off of this, but it does look like somebody had it out to at least scare you. Any idea who might be wanting to do that?"

"Well, I'm not sure. I broke up with my boyfriend eight months ago. He was pretty hot headed and possessive. The other day he saw me having lunch – in the student union – with a donor. Afterward, he came to my office. He was pretty angry and aggressive."

"Since you broke up with him – have you dated him, or called, or anything?"

"No. Nothing. I didn't want anything to do with him anymore, but he apparently has other ideas."

"Did you think of getting a restraining order?"

"I'm not sure there is enough of anything to convince the authorities to give me a restraining order. Besides, I'm not sure it would do much good. And, it might cost him his job."

"If he's doing," Officer Fredericks looked around, "stuff like this, he needs to be stopped. I know it's hard, but if what you say is true, he's not going to give up. He sees you as 'his,' and he means to prove it. What's his name?"

"Robert. Robert Barr."

"Where does he live?"

"Westwood apartments. Number 21. I just can't believe he

would do something like this."

"Anything else happen – that you can think of?"

"No. Wait. I had a flat tire the other night. Late. On the way home. I'd stopped at the market, and about a mile from here, all of a sudden, the tire went pop. A police officer was apparently right behind me. He stayed until the auto club guy arrived to change the tire. Funny, too, because they were brand new – well a few months old, but the tire shouldn't have gone flat. I had to get a new one."

"Let's take a look." Officer Fredericks walked to her car.

"See, the left front is new. A friend of mine took the car and tire to the tire place. The guy at the tire place couldn't fix the flat. So, my friend got a new one to match the others."

Officer Fredericks looked closely at the tire then walked around the car examining each tire carefully. "When did you say you got these?"

"About six months ago. They were supposed to be good tires and they were on sale. Why?"

"Well, first, you don't have a new tire on your car."

"What?"

"You have four new tires. See these little rubber hairs on your tire?"

"Uh huh," said Shannon looking at the left front tire.

"Those little rubber hairs are from the manufacturing process. They only last a short time."

"Well, that just means the tire is new."

"Yes, but all your tires have those little hairs. You've got four new tires. And, I think I know why. These tires are called run-flats. Even with a flat, they don't deflate all the way. You can still drive on them - for a while, anyway. They aren't cheap and I don't think these were on sale. It would appear your friend bought four new tires that would allow you to drive even if you got what would otherwise be a flat tire."

"No. That can't be." Shannon reached into the glove compartment and retrieved a tire warranty folder. She opened it and read the details. "Wait. This can't be."

Twenty

Will walked into the office of the University Weekly. It reminded him of where he'd started out. It seemed a long time ago. The "staff" comprised journalism students. It gave them a chance to work on a paper while they were still in school, learning their trade.

A young man got up from a desk and walked over to him. "Hi. Can I help you?"

"Thank you. My name is Will Daniels, International News Service." Will handed him a card. "I was hoping to talk with the person who wrote the recent story about the motorcycle crash ten years ago."

"Oh. Sure thing. He isn't here right now. Why don't I get the editor, Mr. Daniels?"

"Will. Please."

"Oh. Okay, Will." He said it as if he was privileged to call someone paid as a journalist by his first name. "And I'm Ken. Ken Darling. Please. Don't say it. I hear it enough." Ken ran off to a corner of the room, a small office – probably a former maintenance closet – was where the editor called home.

A young man wearing a gray sweater over a white shirt left the office and walked to Will. "Hi. I'm Jason. Jason Plum. I'm one of the editors. Can I help you?"

Will introduced himself and handed Jason a card. Jason looked impressed but said, "I'm not familiar with International News Service."

"Healthy skepticism. Good trait in a journalist and in an editor," said Will. "Our CEO owns a number of publications and other businesses." Will counted off a half dozen of the magazines published by the firm. "And, some of our stories are published by other magazines and newspapers, as well."

Jason seemed more impressed. "Okay. How can I help?"

"Ten years ago, a motorcycle – and rider – fell short into a canyon. I'd like to talk with the journalist who wrote the piece for the University Weekly."

"Shouldn't be a problem, only he doesn't usually come in until – wait, he just came through the door. Seems it's your lucky day."

Jason motioned to the young man who walked over. "Mark, this is Will Daniels, International News Service. He wants to talk to you about the article you wrote in this week's paper."

"Yeah. Sure. Mark Hanson." Mark reached to shake Will's hand. Will shook it and handed Mark a card.

"Have you got a few minutes to talk, or are you punching in? If you've got time, we could go to the student union."

Jason looked at Mark, shrugged his shoulders and said, "Go ahead."

Will and Mark walked the short distance to the student union.

"So, tell me about the story."

"Well, not really much to tell. Ten years ago, this guy tried to jump a canyon – Snakebite Canyon, actually. Should have known by the name it wasn't a good idea. Anyway, something went wrong, and he plotzed. About twenty feet short – where he landed, anyway. Further out than that if you consider the height he would have had to be at to actually land the thing. It was a miracle that he wasn't killed. Plus, he only spent a couple weeks in the hospital and was released to home. Six months later, he was setting up another jump. Huge crowd at this one."

"Interesting. Could I see your file on the article?"

"Not much of a file, really. I basically used the Northern Coloradoan newspaper accounts. They might be a better source. The paper is pretty thin, ours, that is. We have to pad. Once in a while, we do a "ten years ago today" piece. Just to fill space. Better than writing about a book cart falling over in the library. The accident was the closest thing we could come up with. Since it was just a look back, and I didn't have to do a big article, I just used the Coloradoan files."

Will thanked Mark for the information. Mark asked what Will's path was to his current employment, saying he was looking to make a career in journalism. After that conversation, Will headed downtown to the offices of the Northern Coloradoan.

The offices of the Northern Coloradoan were a bit larger than those of the University Weekly. The atmosphere was more professional, although it was easy to see the staff was overworked. A small paper doesn't make much money, and everybody has a stake in it. Unlike the university paper, if this one folded, people would have trouble paying the rent.

Will introduced himself to the woman at the desk nearest the door. Her name was Mary Clark. She turned out to be the receptionist, proof reader, and ad sales force. He asked if it would be possible to speak to someone who could help him with research on the accident. Mary escorted him to a small ten by ten office in the back. There were two desks, both piled high with papers, a computer, and a business phone. A television in the corner was turned to CNN News. The sound was off.

Mary cleared her throat. A thin man with thinning sand-colored hair, probably in his mid-thirties, turned and looked at Mary, then Will.

Will handed the man a card. "Hi. Will Daniels. International News Service. I know you're busy. I was hoping for a few minutes of your time."

The man stood. "Julius Frank, Mr. Daniels."

"Will, please."

Mary turned and left the room.

"What can I do for you Mr., uh, Will? I don't suppose you're looking to hire someone who will only have to work twelve to fourteen hours a day."

"No. But this reminds me of a place I worked not all that many years ago. Tough job."

"Yes. Tough, but necessary. I still happen to believe that reporting the truth is a sacred duty."

"I'd like to buy you a drink sometime to toast that. Unfortunately, today, I'm looking for some information. About that motorcycle accident at Snakebite Canyon. Any chance I could see the files you have, or talk to the reporter who covered it?"

"You're looking at the reporter who covered it. I've got the files in the cabinet. Mind if I ask why an international news service would be interested in a ten-year-old news story?"

"Good question. I saw the item in the university paper. I thought it was odd, first that they would miscalculate the jump by as much as they did, and second that after hitting the rocks at what was probably seventy-five miles an hour, they guy spent two weeks in the hospital and made another jump six months later."

"And you're interested in this ten years later?"

"Sometimes, I just get a feeling. I think something is, or was, going on that deserves study."

"I always thought so, too. But that group was gone two weeks later. Next time I heard of them, they were in California. Too far for our little paper to investigate, and we stay pretty busy here, just keeping our heads above water. So, it fell off our radar. What do you hope to find?"

"I'm not sure. Maybe a truth that isn't there."

Will spent the next few hours going over the files Julius had as well as the actual articles. He found the rider, Jake Hughes, was a bit of a recluse. Other than just before the jump, he wasn't seen much. Afterward, of course, when he was seen, there were bandages and someone else did the talking. Will thought it strange that someone trying to make money as a flamboyant daredevil would essentially hide himself away. He made a note to check on the second jump in California.

There were few photographs. The ones he had showed a decent sized tent where the motorcycle and gear were kept. There was a runway up to the ramp, which was positioned at the edge of the canyon. On the far side, the place where Jake was supposed to land, there was a rock outcropping to one side. To stop the motorcycle safely, they had piled cardboard boxes to slow and stop the cycle before it hit the rocks.

"Anything interesting?" It was Julius who had approached and looked over Will's shoulder.

"I'm not sure. But it seems there would have been a safer place to make the jump. That rocky outcropping doesn't seem safe. They could have done it where there weren't any rocks and they would have had a smooth runoff area. Why there?" Will looked at his watch. It was getting late, and he wanted to check in with Shannon at work. "Mind if I come back tomorrow and continue?"

"Heck no. Glad for the company. Might pick your brain a little, too. Maybe find a way to make this easier – here." He said it while running his hand through the air to encompass the entire office.

Will headed out the door and back to the university.

Twenty-one

Will entered Shannon's office with more questions than answers. He planned to bounce some of the things he'd found off of her. But when he arrived, she was looking at something on her desk. When she looked up, he could tell she wasn't happy.

"Hi. What's..."

"When were you going to tell me about the run-flats?" Her tone was cold.

"The what?" He was starting to feel queasy.

"The run-flats. You bought run-flats for my car. Five, to be exact. Why?"

"I..."

"Just because I'm a woman doesn't mean I'm stupid and don't know anything about cars and tires. What's the deal?" For once, Shannon felt good being mad. And, it helped cover the fact that until a few hours ago she didn't know anything about run-flats.

"I just wanted you to be safe. I thought about you getting a flat and not being able to get help right away and those seemed safer. Okay. I lied about getting one tire. I didn't want you to..."

"To what! To know about the bullet you found in my tire. I went to the store where you got the tires and talked to man who sold you the five tires you didn't tell me about. Don't you think I should have known about the bullet in my tire? The bullet that caused the flat? If somebody is shooting at me or my car, don't you think you should have told me about that?"

"Okay. I was wrong. I should have told you. I just didn't want you to be scared."

"You wanted me to be stupid? Or maybe innocent. Like a lamb. Being led to slaughter?"

"There was no, no proof if it was intentional. Or of who might have done it."

"Don't you think I should make the decision having to do with my life and my car? What else haven't you told me?"

Will was silent.

"Oh god! What else?!"

"When I took your car to the tire store, I was followed. Blue car. I made turns to see if the car would follow. It did. It passed the tire store before I got out."

"So, I'm being shot at and stalked and you don't think I should know about that? Look, you're going to be gone in a week or two. Someplace far away. You won't be dealing with this. I will. I will. So, if there is anything else, tell me now."

"No. There is nothing else that I know of."

"And you're not going to hide anything else. Are you?"

"No, Ma'am."

"Good. Now that we have that understood, I have work to do." Shannon looked at the papers on her desk. She had nothing that needed to be done, but she wanted to dismiss Will and get control over her emotions.

"Are you going to stay . . ." Will let the question trail off.

"I'll be staying with Sheri for the next couple of nights. I guess I'll see you tomorrow."

Will left the office.

Shannon was still staring at unimportant papers on her desk. She'd have to print them out again. Big teardrops were falling from her eyes, smearing the ink.

Twenty-two

Will Daniels sat at a small round table in the corner of the student union cafeteria. He was facing a window and nursing a cup of coffee. The coffee was more of an excuse to be there than something to drink. He felt like he'd been kicked in the stomach. He'd tried to protect Shannon, but everything she'd said was right. He'd be gone and she would have to deal with whatever it was. Trying to hide the truth from her had only made him look like an ass. Things had been going so well, he was happy about that. Now...

A feminine voice came from behind him. "Pardon me. Is this seat taken?"

Will turned. It was Sheri Chapman. "No. Take your pick. If you've come to gloat, I'd appreciate your sitting elsewhere."

"I haven't come to gloat. Maybe I've come to help."

"Why?"

"Because Shannon is my best friend and until up to about ten o'clock this morning, you made her happy. That all changed when she found out you were hiding information from her."

"I was only – I thought I was only trying to protect her. We didn't have any proof."

"Right. The only problem is, you're going to be gone, leaving her to deal with whatever it is. And protecting her by hiding things that may indicate danger isn't really protecting her."

"I've come to understand that."

"So. No more hiding things from her?

"No."

"No more going behind her back to protect her?"

"No. I've learned my lesson."

"Good. Now. What can I do to protect her?"

Will looked at Sheri. After a moment he said, "Get her to call the Ft. Collins Police Department. Ask for Sergeant Jack Hawkins. He was with us on the ride. Tell him what has happened. They may be able to have a car swing by Shannon's place a few times a night. If Robert is hanging out, it may deter anything stupid he has in mind."

"Okay. Anything else?"

"Is she staying with you?

"Another night or two."

"You might go with her to make sure her house is secure before you leave her for the night. If she'll let you. She could probably use a pepper spray."

"Should she get a gun?"

"No. Two reasons. First, she'd need training, a fair amount of training in order to use it properly. If she doesn't have the training and experience, it could be worse than not having anything at all. Second, even with Robert as a threat, she may hesitate to shoot someone she knows and has had a relationship with. In that case, an enraged Robert might take it and use it against her. Better to have the pepper spray. It's non-lethal. She'll be more likely to use it, and if Robert were to get it, he wouldn't have anything lethal to use against her."

"Okay. Anything else?"

"I don't suppose you can use your magic wand to get me out of trouble."

"Maybe. I'll talk to her."

Twenty-three

Shannon parked her car and walked around to the front of the police station. She entered the glass doors and found herself in the lobby. The décor was spare, but not quite spartan. The desk, behind what was probably bullet-proof glass, was staffed by two uniformed officers. As she approached, they appeared to do a quick scan.

"Yes ma'am. May I help you?" asked one of the officers, a brunette with a nametag that read Simmons.

"Oh, yes. Hi." She was more nervous than she should be. There was a slight shakiness in her legs. "I'd like to talk to someone about problems with an ex-boyfriend. I think he's stalking me."

"What makes you think he's stalking you?"

"Uh," suddenly, her 'proof' didn't seem as iron clad as it had before. "The other night," she started.

Just then, a familiar face appeared behind the desk. Sergeant Hawkins entered through a door and handed the second officer a sheaf of papers. He looked up. "Oh, hi. There's a familiar face. What brings you in today?"

Officer Simmons took ten seconds to brief him.

Hawkins' face darkened. "Why don't you come back to my office? Through the door there." He motioned to the side of the reception desk. An electronic lock buzzed, and Shannon found herself in a small room with a door on the other side. Once the door behind her shut, a second lock buzzer sounded, the door opened, and she walked into the office area.

He escorted her to a small office. The wall facing the corridor was glass, floor to ceiling.

"Please, have a seat. Tell me about the trouble you're having."

"It's really kind of funny. When I came down here, I thought I really had a problem. When the officer – Simmons? – asked me why I thought he was stalking me, I wasn't so sure, all of a sudden."

"Just relax, and tell me. We can decide."

Shannon described Robert's behavior in the office. She also told him about the flat tire and bullet, someone following her car, and the rock through the window.

"Will – Will Daniels, the one who arranged our ride, well he didn't tell me about the bullet. He said there was no proof of who'd shot it. I pretty much blew up at him. Anyway, I decided to come to the station and see if someone – you – thought it was a problem and if it is, what I should do. I thought maybe I should get a gun, but Will said that might be more trouble."

"Actually, yes. That could be more trouble. If you don't know how to use it – in an emergency situation – it could end up being used by your attacker. Smart call. I'll have patrols go by every so often. Maybe have a talk with this guy. There are a couple of other things we might do. Thank you for coming in. Because we only have the outburst in your office – can't really prove the other events yet, it may be a little thin for a restraining order."

"He works at the school, and I don't want to make him lose his job."

"The most important thing is making sure you are safe. Let's see what we can do."

"Thank you, Sergeant. I appreciate anything you can do."

Shannon left the station and drove back to the university.

She had just returned to her office when Sheri entered and walked across the hall to Shannon's office, where she plopped into one of the armchairs in front of Shannon's desk.

"Anything new?"

"I went to the police department – about Robert. I ran into the sergeant who was with us on the motorcycle ride. Where were you?"

"Student union, I wanted to get something to drink."

"I don't suppose you ran into Mr. Daniels."

"Mr. Daniels is it now? As a matter of fact, yes, I did."

"And?"

"At the time, I think he was checking online to figure out how to tie a noose and also where to get some rope. And, I think he was looking for a tree limb to hang himself from."

Shannon gave Sheri a withering look. "Ha, ha."

"Well, maybe not, but he feels really bad. He actually thought he was protecting you – and," Sheri added as Shannon opened her mouth to protest, "he understands he shouldn't have done any of it. He really feels terrible about it. He never wanted to hurt you, you know."

"You sound like you're on his side."

"I'm on both your sides. You're my best friend, and I want what makes you happy."

"But he'll be gone soon – probably back to Clode."

"You know as well as I do that he isn't interested in Clode. And, for as long as he is here, why not enjoy his company. It isn't like there are a lot of guys his level that are hanging around here. And, you never know what might happen. You know. Give the guy another chance. Even if you are right and he's gone in a couple of weeks, you still will have a couple of weeks to – you know."

"I'm not going to 'you know' with him. That's not in the picture. Okay," she continued, "you can let him know he can come back."

"Nope. I've done all my good deeds for today. You're going to have to let him know he can come out of the dog house." With that, Sheri picked herself up and headed back to her office.

Shannon swore under her breath. She picked up her mobile phone and started to send a text. Realizing how impersonal that would be, she dialed Will's number.

"Hello. Shannon?" He'd picked up almost immediately, which made Shannon smile. At least he wasn't playing any hard-to-get games.

"Hi. You understand why I'm upset?"

"Yes. Look, I'm sorry. It was wrong."

"Fine. You might as well come on back in tomorrow morning. I'll see you here."

"Thank you. I . . ."

"Good night. I'll see you in the morning."

"Uh, yeah. Good night."

Shannon hung up. She'd been a little more curt than she needed to be, but she wasn't going to let him off the hook quite yet. Still, the thought of having Will around for a couple of weeks, anyway, made her smile.

Twenty-four

Robert Barr hid in a small group of bushes on the corner of Shannon's property. He was well hidden. Shannon had returned home an hour ago. Robert thought about approaching the home, maybe just to look in and see what she was doing, but he'd noticed police cars cruising through the neighborhood. They weren't on a regular routine, just randomly, and he couldn't be sure if another would come by while he was looking in a window. If this continued, he wouldn't be able to watch Shannon at home. That made him mad.

A patrol car passed the house. Robert waited until it was gone, then came out of the bushes and walked down the sidewalk and across the street. His car was parked around the corner. He got into his car, started it, and headed home, driving past Shannon's house, curious to see any hint of her. A block later, flashing lights came on behind him.

"Shit! Now WHAT!"

A rather large looking policeman dismounted his motorcycle and walked to Robert's car. He stood just behind the window post, a place where he could clearly see Robert, but where Robert couldn't see him well. It was a position safest for the officer when making a stop.

"Evening officer. Was I doing something wrong?"

"License and registration, sir."

"Was I doing something wrong?" Robert pulled his license out of his wallet with some difficulty. He realized his hand was shaking as he handed it to the policeman. "The registration is in the glove compartment. May I get it?" Robert didn't want to make any mistakes.

"Sure." The area of the glove compartment was illuminated with a flashlight.

Robert pulled out the registration and handed it out to the policeman. He cursed his shaking hand.

The officer studied the documents, then walked to the back

of the car. Robert was wondering if he should make a run for it, but realized that would be stupid. Besides, they didn't really have anything on him.

The officer returned. He handed the documents back to Robert. "Just routine, Mr. Barr. We've had some vandalism and reports of unknown persons apparently looking for opportunities. Do you know a woman by the name of Shannon Sullivan?"

"Uh, yeah, yes. Why?" He wanted to lie, but the lie could be checked, and he didn't want to be caught in a lie by the police.

The police officer paused noticeably. "Miss Sullivan has indicated a few incidents of vandalism, and in our interview, your name came up. Would you happen to know anything about any vandalism involving Miss Sullivan?"

"Uh, no. No. Really." Now, he was really sweating.

"You can go, Mr. Barr. You should know that we are going to continue looking into these incidents and will be very interested if any additional acts of vandalism occur."

"Yes, sir. I have, um, no idea about these, uh, incidents. May I go, officer .. ?"

"Hawkins. Sergeant Hawkins."

Robert drove off, making sure to keep his speed down below the speed limit and his acceleration moderate. His hands shook on the wheel, and sweat ran down his face. *Well, shit! I can't come back here. Not only will they have patrol cars, but they know who I am and where I live. I get caught here again, and there may be real trouble. I'll have to get her at school. Man! That was close.*

Twenty-five

Shannon walked down the hall to her office. The office was dark. As she opened the door and entered, sensors automatically turned on half of the lights in the ceiling. The small room behind the main office was also dark. Shannon felt her spirits drop. She tried to ask herself why, but she knew why. Despite having 'a talk' with Will the day before, she hoped he would be in the office waiting for her.

She noticed a white paper bag on her desk. She started to reach for it when the office phone rang. Shannon jumped.

"Hi!" it was Sheri, across the hallway. Shannon was so focused on her office, she hadn't even noticed Sheri was already in. And, sitting with a cup of coffee and a pastry. "Mine's cherry. I'm betting yours is cheese."

"What?"

"I think Will was here early. Not too early. The coffee is still hot."

Shannon opened the bag. There was an insulated cup, she guessed with coffee, and what was probably a pastry wrapped in paper.

"So. Do I win the bet? Cheese?"

It was a cheese Danish. "Some bet. Ever since you told him, I've been getting these regularly."

"Good thing I told him the truth, otherwise, you'd be getting PB and J with pickles. Is there a note?"

Inside Shannon's bag was a note saying that Will hoped she had a good day and that he needed to check files at the newspaper office – the Northern Coloradoan, not the university paper.

"He went to the paper to look at some files. Note also says he should be back, maybe by lunch, if I am available."

"That sounds promising."

"Shush!" said Shannon, popping the top on the coffee and unwrapping a somehow still warm Danish. "If I call the paper and say I'm available, it makes me sound like I'm anxious and needy. If I don't call ..."

"You may blow your chance to have lunch and dinner, and maybe a follow-up breakfast after the dinner."

"Sheri, sometimes I wonder just what runs around in that head of yours."

"So, you call, you feel needy. You don't call, you seem like you don't care. What's a good middle ground? Wait! Here's an idea. Head down to the paper. You're just going by to see what he's found out. It makes it more about the investigation than about him. As long as you're there, you might as well go to lunch together. The B&B can come later."

Shannon just rolled her eyes. "Well, the least I can do is finish my coffee and Danish." She hung up her phone.

Sheri came across the hall and into her office. "Yes. It would be such a shame to let it go to waste." She said it as she was taking the last bite of her Danish. She plopped into a chair and sipped her coffee.

"I don't want to go running down there and make it look like I'm desperate."

"Of course not. You've got guys lining up in the hallway. You'll have to fight your way through the crowd before you can head down there."

"Shush! You're such a buzz kill." Shannon sagged slightly in her seat, realizing that while not desperate, there wasn't a horde of men she would want to spend her life with. "I hate it when you're right. But, better alone than with someone like Robert. Once you're out of school and living in a college town ..."

They sat and chatted while Sheri finished her coffee and Shannon finished both her coffee and Danish. "God! Where does he get these things! I've never found anything this good anywhere in the city. Maybe it's a good thing I don't know."

Shannon made sure there was nothing emergent, packed a few things in her purse, and headed to the paper's office. She'd been there a few times before and knew the editor. When she entered the office, he greeted her and showed her to where Will Daniels was set up.

"Oh, hi. You didn't have to come all the way down here."

"You seemed to be making some headway, and I was curious about what you'd found." Shannon had worked on a number of responses on the way to the paper. She hoped this one sounded reasonable. When Will turned away from her, she bit her lip lightly, like a teenager hoping the line would work.

"Yeah." Will hurriedly cleared documents from a second chair in the office. "Please, have a seat." He then turned to the files.

"Okay. So, who is the most famous person to make motorcycle jumps?" he asked.

Shannon thought a few seconds and said, "Evel Knievel."

"Right. And we know a lot about him. We know where he was born, who his parents were, who his grandparents were. We know he served in the Army, rode motocross from early ages, sold insurance, worked in a mine. We know all that stuff. We know absolutely nothing about Jake Hughes. Mr. Frank has a pretty extensive file on him and the jump. I guess it's been a mild obsession. As far as he can tell, Jake Hughes didn't exist before he made that first jump."

"Well, but later. Didn't he make more jumps. Somebody must have interviewed him, found out where he was from."

"That's the thing. He didn't really grant any interviews. He kept pretty much to himself. And, that seems to be odd behavior for a guy who wants to promote himself as a daredevil."

"Maybe he changed his name – you know, so he could bury his past."

"Possible, but with the notoriety of the crash somebody should have recognized him – unless he needed extensive facial reconstruction; but he was only in the hospital a couple of weeks. Anyway, Evel Knievel even did some jail time. Unless this guy is a wanted murder suspect who changed his name and face, it doesn't make sense."

Will looked through the documents and pulled out another sheet. "Six months later, he tries the same stunt. This time, because of the first failure, he has a lot more sponsors – everybody wants to see a daredevil killed in the attempt . . ." Will gave a wry smile in response to the shocked look on Shannon's face. "Anyway, there was a lot more money. This time, he did it in another location. About the same distance, less of a fall if he doesn't make it. But he did. Make it. After that, there were eight jumps in the next five years. Each time, he made more money."

"That means," Shannon started slowly, "he'd need a social security number to get paid. Oh, wouldn't he have to fill out some kind of paperwork in order to make the jump? I mean, depending where he was, there would have to be forms. There are <u>always</u> forms."

"Yeah. Great idea. We can check with city hall for a start."

Shannon smiled, happy that she had come up with something Will might not have considered.

"You know, if you keep this up, I may have to hire you," he said.

"You might not be able to afford me," Shannon replied in a deadpan manner, then smiled.

Will laughed. "You're right. Why don't we grab some lunch?"

Twenty-six

"Do you really think people watch things like motorcycle jumps to see the rider get killed?" asked Shannon.

They were sitting in a small modern contemporary restaurant a few blocks from the paper. Shannon had opted for a scallop salad. Will had ordered the ahi tuna salad. They each sipped a glass of pinot grigio.

"Well, one of the reasons people go to car races is to see the crashes. Stands to reason . . ."

"I didn't think you were the cynical type."

"I try not to be, but in many of the stories I've done, let's just say I found human behavior to be somewhat less than – well, human."

"So, what are you going to do next?"

"I'll keep looking through the stuff at the paper. He's got some negatives – from photos that were taken. I'm going to have those printed. I'll study those. You never know what you'll find. I'd also like to see what I can find out about the next jump or two he did. It's just odd that there is no record of this guy doing anything on motorcycles before the first jump – a two hundred-footer at that. Evel Knievel's first jump was only twenty feet. And, he almost missed that one. So, for a guy to come out of nowhere and make – well, try – a jump of two hundred feet, it boggles the mind."

"Okay. I guess I'll take your word on that."

"I'd like to take a look at the jump site, too. Do you know where it is?"

"Yes. Well, not exactly, but I know the area. I'm sure I could find the exact spot. I think."

"Well, the photographs should help pinpoint it. I'll see if they are ready this afternoon. Maybe I can at least get the ones that would help find the site. We could head over together – if that works into your schedule."

The silver SUV sped along the two-lane asphalt road toward

the site of Jake Hughes first motorcycle jump. The destination was in a park about fifty miles from town. Shannon was looking at the photographs she and Will had picked up at the photo shop. Shannon knew the general location, but it might take some time to find the exact location. She wanted to find the exact spot. She didn't think Will was going to find anything useful, but she wanted to get the right spot. Just in case it actually was important.

"So, I think the jump site shouldn't be too far from the parking areas. Doesn't make sense to make spectators walk too far."

"Maybe they wanted to limit the number of spectators. It seems like the whole thing was done to avoid a lot of publicity, unbelievable as that sounds. I mean, why do a jump if people aren't going to see it?" Will seemed lost in thought, then, "unless..."

"Unless what?" asked Shannon.

"Oh, I'm sorry. I guess I was thinking out loud. I was thinking unless they didn't want many spectators. Just a few. But that just raises another set of questions. It is like putting on a play and not selling tickets."

"That doesn't make any sense," said Shannon.

"Like I said before. The whole thing is just odd."

Shannon was quiet for a minute. "So, as long as we have a few minutes, tell me about your job, your office. Where do you live? I don't know any of that."

"Job? Oh, as I said before, I'm a journalist. I work for an international news agency. I spend a fair amount of time on the road, as they say. Mostly Europe and some in North America. Occasionally, South America. I've got to admit, I love my work. I travel. I love to learn things and write about them. My work is my life. The main office is in Paris. As I said, I have an apartment there. More than I really need, but I like to have some space."

"Paris? Is that where 'Clode' works?"

"Clode? Oh, yeah. She does stories on fashion for the agency, as well as fashion shows and industry trends. Why does Clode interest you?"

"Just wondering. When she called, Sheri said she seemed to have her nose stuck up in the air."

"Yes. She can be, how should I say, superior in her attitude. She's also Parisian, which makes her act as if she's superior to everyone else on the planet."

"And the stories? The ones you do?"

"Sometimes they assign a story to me. Sometimes I go to them with something I think will be of interest. That's what I did here. The more we learn, the weirder this whole thing seems. Before this trip, I had to do a story on the Swedish women's volleyball team."

"I can see how that must have been 'above and beyond the call of duty.'" Shannon was staring out the passenger window so she wouldn't let Will see the smile on her face. She was trying to put on a judgmental facade. Smiling at the same time would have killed the guise.

"Yeah. Everybody says that. But trust me, it wasn't quite as much fun as you imagine. My small room was miles from theirs. They were only available two hours a day, and they weren't terribly interested or cooperative when they were present. Actually, they made Clode look like the friendly girl next door."

"Still," she said.

"Years ago, I covered a story about terrorists in Spain."

Shannon noticed that he suddenly seemed lost in thought. She spotted the turnoff.

"Oh. I think this is it. Pull in here."

Will turned into a parking lot, about twenty yards on each side. Gravel crunched beneath the tires. "Not very big – for such an event."

Twenty-seven

The crunch of the gravel lot continued as Will pulled the SUV to a creosote impregnated log that acted as a parking boundary. He turned off the engine an opened his door. The scene outside was arid. And warm. Occasional outcroppings of rocks, some as small as two feet high, some ten or fifteen, dotted the land. Scrub oaks and grasses, as well as small bushes dotted the area. Although actually filled with life, the landscape gave the impression of being barren.

"Looks kind of desolate," he said.

"I don't know. I grew up in this part of the country. It's what I'm used to. There isn't much water around here, so the plant life and animals have had to adapt. If you're here for any length of time, you'll find it has a beauty all its own."

Will was skeptical, but kept his opinion to himself. He looked around to determine the path to the river, to start the search.

"I should probably lead the way. Good thing I changed into walking shoes and out of those heels I was wearing."

"Why should you lead the way?" he asked.

"I'm more familiar with the land. And other things you might not be aware of."

"Like?"

"Like the rattlesnake sunning itself over there." Shannon laughed.

Will's head snapped in the direction Shannon had pointed. Sure enough, a large snake was on the rocks about forty feet from where they were standing. "Jesus! You think there are more of them?"

"Probably. We'll just have to keep an eye out."

"There doesn't seem to be a path."

"No, but the river is this way," she said pointing diagonally from where they were standing.

"How do you know? It all looks the same."

"Well, stands to reason. The road is back there. River wouldn't be there. Besides, I've got a compass. We'll walk to the river bank then walk along until we come to the spot where he made the jump."

"And the snakes?"

"Best to avoid those. When we spot one, we'll give it wide berth."

"And the ones we don't spot?"

"They usually rattle before the strike. We'll let him, or her, know they won, back away, and give them wide berth, too."

"Anything else?"

"No. The mountain lions usually stay up in the hills. Same with the bears, although we do see them from time to time. Wolves don't usually bother people. Biggest problem might be getting assaulted by a buck in heat." Shannon was smiling at his discomfort. It was nice having him out of his element. "We'll be fine. Just enjoy yourself."

They started off in the direction Shannon had indicated.

Will's head was turning quickly left to right and back. He was trying his best to look nonchalant, but his concern showed. "Wouldn't there be a trail, or road, they would have followed?"

"People don't come out here very often. Probably the reason there wasn't much of a fight when it was proposed as a park, a hundred years ago. When people do come, they walk where they want. They just enjoy being here. It isn't a place where you have a path to 'the' spectacular overlook. The guys who did the jump probably trucked stuff in – around the rocks and trees and over the grass and brush. After ten years, nothing left to tell where."

Will saw something in the grass off to the left. After making sure it didn't look like a snake, he went over and picked it up. It was a beer can with six bullet holes in it.

"Oh yeah. Folks do that, too," she said.

They walked on, Shannon leading the way. Will finally caught up and walked beside her. He was continually scanning for snakes. He figured he could spot a deer – or worse – without any trouble. They finally arrived at the river. Will thought the term river was a bit of an overstatement. The water was only about ten or fifteen feet wide. He'd grown up in the St. Louis area. The Missouri and Mississippi Rivers made this not worth mentioning.

"Not much of what I would call a river," he said.

"This is the dry season. When the rains come and the snow melts, it will be different story. Maybe not much by your standards, but the little bit of water in this river has been fought over and caused violent deaths for more than a hundred years. Water is life. And, here," she gestured at the landscape in front of them, "it is scarce."

Will looked at Shannon. Before, he'd seen her as a beautiful woman, probably very competent in her job. Now, he saw her as someone more. She knew the history of her land. She knew the nature, the politics, and the history. She'd also given it a lot of thought. There was a lot more to her than he'd discovered. He wondered how much more this young woman was.

"I'm not sure," she said, shaking him out of his thoughts, "but it looks like the cliff gets higher if we go that way," she gestured to the right. "The other way, it looks like it flattens out."

"You've done great so far. And, I haven't been bitten by a snake, so lead on."

"You do know this is called Snakebite Canyon – right?"

"Don't remind me."

They walked along the canyon rim, checking spot after spot. Finally, after an hour, Shannon and Will looked at the photographs they had an decided they were on the take-off side of the canyon, at the right location. Straight across was where the motorcycle should have landed.

"Wow. He thought he was going to make this?" she asked.

"Yeah. Two hundred feet across. Then, there's the drop."

Will and Shannon peered over the edge of the canyon to the rocks on the other bank.

"I don't get it. High risk. Low reward."

"Okay," said Shannon, "you've made me a believer. I don't see how he survived. It looks a lot worse here than it did in the pictures."

Will walked around, took some pictures and made some measurements. "I'd love to get to the other side. See? There is the rock outcropping. The only one for at least a hundred yards, yet they chose this spot. It seems like the rock would have been a major hazard. It must have served some purpose. Maybe to hide something behind it. Nobody but crew were allowed over there." He took photos of the rocks Jake had landed on. "Any way to get over there?"

"A couple," Shannon responded. "Go the long way around. A fjord, most likely, probably ten miles that way." She pointed in the direction they had come. "Get your pretty SUV all dirty. And, it would take about four hours or more. Dark by then. If you have money, you could hire a helicopter. Seems expensive for what you'd find."

"Anything else?"

"Well," she said with a smile, "if you'd been born over there, it would be easier." Then, she laughed.

Will shook his head. Then smiled. He pulled out his phone and checked their location. He wrote that down in his notebook.

"What are you doing?"

"Putting down the coordinates. Somebody must have a drone. If I can get someone to fly it out here, I can get photos without getting my feet wet so to speak."

The sun was approaching the horizon when they reached the SUV in the parking lot.

Will opened Shannon's door. "Thank you."

"Just because you pretty much bested me in everything we did this afternoon doesn't mean you shouldn't be treated like the lady you are."

"There should be more men like you around. And, I'm not sure you were 'bested.' You're just out of your realm. But if anyone suggested to my former boyfriend that he should open or hold a door for me he'd either stare at them or laugh outright."

"Too bad. He sounds like a real schmuck. You deserve better. I know you're competent, intelligent, and capable of opening your own doors. I just think a little courtesy makes the day more pleasant. Unless you mind. But if you did, I think you would have said something."

"No. I don't mind. It feels nice to be treated," Shannon paused. She wanted to use the right word. She didn't want him to think she didn't appreciate his gestures. At the same time, she didn't want him to think just holding a door was going to make her melt. "Courteously," she finally decided on.

The ride home took an hour and a half. Shannon looked tired, so Will told her to recline the seat, which she did. When he covered her with a coat he had in the back seat, she curled into it and rolled onto her left side. She tried to watch him for a while, but soon, her eyes closed and her breathing deepened.

Will drove, thinking about the woman in his past – Ariel. And what had happened. He glanced at Shannon. She was, in some ways, so like her. The pain of his loss had subsided, but not the belief that somehow, he was responsible. He shouldn't have kept information from Shannon, but he'd found he wanted to protect her – to make sure she was never hurt.

They arrived at Shannon's well after dark. Will pulled into the drive and stopped as carefully as he could. Shannon woke with the light jolt. Still half asleep, she said, "I'm sorry. I slept through the entire ride. I guess I'm not much of a guest."

"You're the perfect guest. Let me walk you to the door and make sure everything is secure." He got out of the SUV, walked to her side, opened the door and helped her out. She took his arm as they walked to the front door. Shannon opened the door and they entered.

"Do you mind if I check to make sure everything's okay?"

Shannon thought it was overkill but answered, "No. Go ahead." She felt safe with this man. She would ask him to stay but she didn't want to send the wrong signal – well, at least not yet.

Will returned in a couple of minutes. "Everything seems safe.

Back door is secure. I'll wait to leave until I hear you lock this one."

Shannon leaned over and kissed him softly on the lips. "Thank you for a very nice day."

"Yeah. We didn't get bitten by a snake, fall off a cliff, or anything." Then, "Do you want me to pick you up in the morning? Your car is still at the paper."

"I'll call Sheri. It's about time she did something. Besides, with us together all afternoon and evening, I'm sure she'll want an update."

"Well, good night then. I enjoyed your company very much."

They kissed again, this time longer and not quite as softly. Will stepped onto the porch and waited for the sound of Shannon locking the door. He drove to his hotel and took a hot shower. Just before bed, he saw a text on his phone. 'Thank you again. Wonderful time. Sleep tight. S' He sent back, 'The wonderful time was because of you. Sweet dreams. Tomorrow. W'

Shannon rolled onto her side and wrapped herself around her body pillow. She squeezed it tightly and had a smile on her face.

Twenty-eight

Shannon and Sheri sat in the front seats of Sheri's car, which was parked in Shannon's drive. The engine was running, but the transmission was in 'Park.'

"Um, are we going to go?" asked Shannon.

"Sure. Just as soon as you tell me what happened yesterday. And, why you need a ride. Did he just leave? Were you afraid of the 'walk of shame,' if you rode in with him?"

"It wasn't that way." Shannon tried to pull off an indignant look and tone. Sheri wasn't buying it.

"I'm sure it wasn't. But let's see. You had coffee and Danish in the office, then, you left to see – well, pretend to see, how his research was going. And, maybe lunch. But you didn't return after lunch. Then, no Shannon before I left – I worked until seven last night, by the way. Oh, and when I turned on my phone this morning, I had a text from you asking me to pick you up this morning. Again, did he just leave? Or is he looking at us through the blinds and his car is parked around the corner?"

"Where do you come up with these ideas? Drive, and I'll talk."

Sheri backed out of the drive. When she got to the street, she stopped and scanned the house one more time."

"He's not there. He wasn't there. I slept in my own bed – alone."

"Sadder words were never spoken. So, no dirty dancing?"

"No. I went to the paper. He showed me some of the files he was looking at. Then, he said he wanted to see some pictures . . ."

"Naked pictures?"

Shannon gave Sheri a disapproving look. Sheri shrugged her shoulders and said, "Would spice up the story."

"Of the crash site. He'd sent the negatives to be printed – eight by tens. While we waited for the pictures, we had lunch at that restaurant on Pine – the Blue Cactus. Before you ask, seafood salads, one glass of wine, opposite sides of the table."

Sheri gave Shannon a look that said, 'big deal.' "How was the food?"

"Excellent, actually. After lunch, we got the photos. Will said he wanted to check the real site – in person. I decided to go along, to keep him from getting lost – you know."

"I wonder if he bought that any more than I did."

"Actually, a good thing I did. I don't think he knows anything about the great American west outdoors. Took us about an hour to get there. He thought the scenery was bleak."

"Except when he was looking at you, probably. God! I hope it wasn't *while* he was looking at you!"

"You're enjoying this, aren't you?"

"Just trying to make it fun."

"It took a while to find the actual spot. He missed seeing a couple of rattlesnakes. They weren't close, but still. I'd hate to think of him getting bitten, especially out there alone. Was kinda funny though, him scanning the ground constantly, sure he was going to step on a rattler."

"Yes. With nobody to suck out the poison; depending where the snake actually bit him. You were referring to the snake biting him, right?"

"I feel like I'm back in junior high school having this conversation at a pajama party. I would say back in high school, but by then, our conversations were a bit more mature."

"You said bit," Sheri giggled.

Shannon dropped her head against the headrest, rolled her eyes and said, "God!"

"Sorry. Continue."

"By the time we got back to the SUV, the sun was heading toward sunset.

Sheri parked her car. "Where's yours?"

"Still at the paper. I can get it later." She looked at Sheri, "Stop!"

Sheri shrugged.

I kind of fell asleep on the way home. He covered me with his coat on the ride. We got home, he checked to make sure everything was okay, and we kissed good night."

"Whoops! Back it up. I want to know everything – and I mean everything about those last four words."

Shannon explained about the kisses. The explanation, thanks to about forty questions from Sheri, took ten times longer than the actual kisses. "You know," she finished, "next time we kiss, why don't I invite you over. It will save a lot of time and explanation."

Sheri gave Shannon an "Oh MY!" look and cocked one eye. Shannon regretted saying what she had.

"So," said Sheri, "why didn't you invite him in for coffee? You know – c-o-f-f-e-e – wink, wink, nudge, nudge."

"Well, it HAS been a long time since I've had any 'coffee.' Tell you the truth, before Robert, I didn't have 'coffee' all that much. Like now, I guess, too much time in the library. Anyway, 'coffee' with Robert wasn't worth it. It was like a race to see how fast he could finish . . ."

"His coffee."

"Right. At first, I wanted him to stay and hold me. You know, the way you do after 'coffee.' It didn't take long before I was glad to have him gone. And, I started making up excuses why I didn't want 'coffee.' Headache. Once a month, you know, I didn't want 'coffee' at all. And, the week before that, well, I became hard to live with. Sometimes it worked. Sometimes, he didn't care. 'Coffee' with Robert, though not frequent, became a meaningless chore."

"Wow! I just got a picture of a big smelly beast ripping off your clothes and doing something you would only suffer through."

"Even that would have been more romantic. The last time Robert tried to have 'coffee' with me it was at a party, on a bed full of coats, and I had a button poking me in the back of the head." Shannon paused. "Anyway, yes, Will kissed me. But, I'm not ready for 'coffee' yet."

"You sure? Sounds to me like what you really need is some fresh, strong coffee. Something that will jolt you. Something ..."

"Run out of ways to do the coffee metaphor?"

"From your description of life with Robert, maybe we shouldn't ever use the word coffee again."

Twenty-nine

Will Daniels arrived about ten o'clock. Sheri was sitting in one of Shannon's arm chairs sipping a diet soft drink.

"Hi! In the mood for coffee?" he asked.

Sheri coughed and spewed soda out her nose and all over herself and Shannon's desk.

"You okay?" he asked

"It's nothing. She must have gotten it down the wrong tube. Sometimes she gets sensitive about coffee. Why don't we go to the student center? While Sheri cleans up."

Ten minutes later, Shannon and Will sat in the student center cafeteria. Will was sipping his coffee. Shannon had opted for tea.

"I'm having the rest of the negatives from the paper printed. There are about twenty or so."

"You expect to see something else?"

"Hard to tell. You never know what the photographer might have caught. Sometimes, seemingly worthless pictures have something in one corner. You know, like Bigfoot, or something."

"Yes, except we haven't found one with a picture of Bigfoot in the corner."

"True. I'd love to get a copy of the actual film of the jump. The local television station had a crew there. I wonder if they would be willing to make or part with a copy."

"Local station?"

"Yeah. They did the filming. I guess the Denver station thought if anything notable happened, they could get a copy from the affiliate. They didn't think it was worth it to send a crew."

"Then, as it turns out . . ."

"Exactly. I wonder who I call. Do you know the station manager?" he asked.

"Oh, yes. And, I think I can be of some help to you there. Mind if I tag along?"

"Not at all. I'd love to have your company."

"I just need to make one call first." Shannon stood and walked away from the table. She pulled her phone out of her bag and punched a few numbers. "Hi. This is Shannon Sullivan. Right." Shannon was walking away, and that was all Will heard before Shannon's words became too quiet to hear. She turned and started walking back to the table. "Great. I appreciate it. Thank you." She closed the call and turned to Will. "All set. Oh, wait." Shannon walked away from the table again for another call. She returned less than a minute later.

"What was that?"

"Just a little something to help you get what you want. And, I wanted to be sure the station manager had a few minutes."

They walked to Will's SUV. A groundskeeper was cutting the grass, his hat flopping over his face and neck, covering them from the sun. "Well, isn't that sweet," hissed Robert from under his floppy hat, "holding her door and everything. A real gentleman." Robert stared after the SUV long after it had gone. There was anger in his eyes. Anger and hate.

They got into the vehicle and Will pulled out of the spot, heading in the direction Shannon indicated. A few minutes later, Will's SUV turned in to the parking lot of the local television station. As soon as they entered, Will could see it was run professionally.

A receptionist greeted them. "Good morning. May I help you?"

"Hi. Yes," responded Shannon. She introduced herself. "I spoke with Mr. Martel a few minutes ago. He's expecting us."

The receptionist picked up her phone and checked with the person on the other end. Then to Shannon and Will, "Please come this way." They followed her to a contemporary office. Inside, a man in shirtsleeves and tie. He rose from the desk and walked to the door.

"Shannon. What a nice surprise. It's so good to see you. And your friend?"

"Daniels, sir. Will Daniels. International News Service." Will handed him a card.

"Impressive. What is it that our little television station has that could be of interest to you or your organization?" He said it with a smile, but Will thought there was a little what's-in-it-for-me hiding behind the smile.

"Ten years ago, a guy tried to jump a 200-foot canyon. He came up a bit short."

"Yes. I remember it well."

"There was film taken at the time. I'm hoping to locate the film and maybe get a lead on finding who shot it."

"Well, to take care of the second first. I shot the film. I have to admit, I kind of lost it when I saw the guy disappear under the cliff face. Shaky film running to the edge. Then, we saw him twisted in the wreckage of the bike. I still can't believe he lived – and with only minor injuries. Why the interest ten years later?"

"I saw the piece in the university paper. It piqued my interest. As I started looking into it, I couldn't believe the guy lived, either. I'm hoping to find out what I can from the film."

"Uh, yeah. It should be in our archives. Probably take some time to find exactly where it is."

"How about if I provide some incentive?" asked Shannon.

"Incentive?" asked the two men in unison.

"Yes, Charles," she said looking at the station manager. "If you can find it by tomorrow, I've got four tickets in the President's box for the Wyoming game."

Will saw Charles' eyes open wide.

"President's box? Wyoming game?"

"I'm sure there would be someone you'd like to impress."

"Uh, well, uh, I can take a look – tonight – and get back to you first thing in the morning." He was playing coy, but not doing very well.

Shannon handed him her business card. "We r-e-a-l-l-y appreciate it. I was able to get the tickets, and I can't think of anyone I'd rather give them to."

Will and Shannon made their goodbyes and headed for the door. On their way out they heard Charles say, "I'll be in archives for the rest of the day. I don't want to be bothered."

"So, you want to tell me about your magic?" asked Will.

"Easy. I have friends. They get me tickets. In this case, tickets he'd kill to get. President's box for the Wyoming game is about as good as it gets around here. He can invite people he wants to impress in the community. It'll be good – make that great – for him and the station."

"A football game?"

"Yeah. You'd be surprised. Not a fan?"

"Gave it up years ago. I've got better things to do with my time."

Well, she thought, *depending what other things those were, it was a good sign – for a man.*

Thirty

Will sat in the library media room watching the film of the failed jump on his computer. The station manager sent a digital copy – he said he didn't want to release the only original. Will ran the video over and over. He'd made some measurements based on the length on the motorcycle and other objects in the film, to determine the length of the ramp itself. Then, he used the timer on his phone to determine the length of time the motorcycle was on the ramp. He measured it twenty times, but it came up the same. The absolute fastest the motorcycle could have been going when it left the ramp was seventy miles per hour – ten miles per hour slower than would have been needed to complete the jump successfully.

Will sat back and stared at the ceiling. None of it made any sense. He sighed and decided to run what he'd found past Shannon. He walked out of the media room, down a hallway, and up one level to the administrative offices. He stopped at the end of the hallway. Shannon was at her desk, engrossed in some paperwork. He looked at her red hair and pale skin. He thought he was coming to talk about the research. He realized he was actually coming for another reason. Just seeing her made him feel happy. There was a tingle inside him. The universe was pulling him toward her. But then, too, there was work. His work was his life – maybe he needed his work. After Ariel, work had become his way of blocking out anything that could hurt him. Maybe he needed work more than he suspected.

Will looked in the door, and quietly knocked. Shannon looked up and motioned for him to enter.

"Hi. What's up?"

"I've been looking at the film of the event." They'd decided to use the word 'event.' They could have used the word 'jump,' but each time they'd tried, they'd corrected to 'attempted jump,' and they decided it was a distraction. So, 'event' became the description.

"And?"

"And, it makes no sense. I've done measurements over and over. The fastest the motorcycle could have been going when it left the ramp was about seventy miles an hour. That wasn't fast enough to make the jump successfully. I mean, just looking at the same jump done by Evel Knievel would have told them the bike would have to be going eighty. The rider made two run-ups. That's to check that the bike is working and can get the needed speed."

"So, if he wasn't going fast enough, why try the jump?"

Will just looked at Shannon.

"Maybe," she said, "he thought the bike was working when it wasn't."

"Wait. What you're saying is that – that – the speedometer was off? I would think that would be one of the things they would have made sure of. That makes almost less sense than jumping at too slow a speed."

"Unless," Shannon continued, "the person making the jump didn't know the speedometer was off."

"You're suggesting that the speedometer was tampered with – to make the rider think the bike was going fast enough? That wouldn't just be a mistake. That would be a deliberate change to make whoever was on the bike think everything was okay when it wasn't. THAT would be – in this case, attempted murder."

"Well," Shannon said, "in the words of Sherlock Holmes, 'When you've eliminated the impossible, whatever is left, however improbable, is the truth.' In this case, going up the ramp, the rider apparently thought he had enough speed to make the jump. If you also believe that he knew just how much speed he needed – and that he wasn't suicidal, you're left with failure of the speedometer – in the exact amount needed to convince the rider he would make it, or that someone deliberately tampered with the mechanism to get the result they got."

Will pondered what she'd said. "What you're suggesting is monstrous. Deliberately send someone to certain grave injury – or death. Unfortunately, what you say also makes some sense – logically. I still cannot imagine someone would do that. But, after six months, how would he get back on the bike and make an almost identical jump?"

"Hey," she said, "I've solved enough of your mystery for one day. That's all you get. If you want more help, you'll have to come back later."

Will was having trouble concentrating. Not only was he thinking about what she'd suggested, he was mesmerized by the beautiful green eyes that were looking at him. *Pale skin. Little freckles. Red hair. Intelligent. Beautiful.*

"Did you hear me? You seem to be somewhere else."

"Uh, yeah, no. I'm sorry. Oh, are you free for dinner?"

Shannon tilted her head slightly. She wasn't sure where his mind had gone for those few seconds. "Um, sure. Give me an hour. We can figure it out then."

Will rose from the chair and went to say something. His tongue tangled somewhat. He finally said, "Sure. About an hour." He looked at her a little longer, then finally turned and left, feeling like a high school freshman who had just tried to ask a girl to the prom.

After Will left, Shannon buzzed Sheri and asked her to come over.

Sheri plopped into one of Shannon's office chairs. "What's up?"

Shannon described Will's visit. She talked a little about the event, but told Sheri about Will's trouble communicating. "He seemed to space out for a while. It was strange. I felt a bit concerned."

"Sounds to me," said Sheri, "that someone is smitten."

"I'm not smitten. It was just strange."

"Not sayin' it was you who is smitten."

"What? No. I mean, he is . . ."

"Gorgeous, intelligent, gentile, stop me before I get to heart-thumpingly-hot. Still, you're gorgeous, intelligent, and heart-thumpingly-hot in your own right. Give me a minute to imagine what your children are going to look like."

"Sheri, I swear to god!"

"What? Don't think it's possible? You're a beautiful woman. And smart. The combination scares a lot of guys who are afraid they aren't good enough. But he is smart and not threatened by a strong, intelligent woman, who by the way, is also beautiful."

"Round, spotted, and pale."

"When I saw you two the other day, I thought I saw something in his eyes. Women can be deceptive. Men give themselves away with their eyes all the time. I saw something smoldering."

"I just can't believe – I mean, he's a world traveler. His life is so much more than . . ."

"Than the small-town girl who thinks she was lucky to get a job in a university library and thinks there aren't any men interested in her?"

Shannon sat back, "I . . ."

"Shannon's got a boyfriend. Shannon's got a boyfriend. Shannon's got a boyfriend."

Shannon picked up an empty paper cup and threw it at Sheri.

Thirty-one

Will Daniels stood in the men's room facing the mirror. He splashed water on his face and used paper towels to dry himself. *For crying out loud. Try not to make a complete fool of yourself. You're not in middle school.* He took a deep breath, let it out, and headed for the door. But he knew he hadn't felt this way about any woman since losing Ariel and burying himself in his work. It both excited and terrified him.

Shannon sat at her desk. She was trying not to think of what Sheri had said. She felt nervous, then chided herself for feeling nervous. She wasn't sure what they were going to do for dinner. She knew if she could get through dinner, she could head home and have the night to ponder Sheri's idea. Speaking of Sheri, she had been missing for the last two hours and just said she'd be back.

There was a quiet knock. Will was at the door. Shannon's heart raced and she felt her face flush. *Sheri! If she hadn't said what she did, I wouldn't be feeling like this.* "Oh, Hi! Come on in."

Will entered her office. Shannon thought he looked a little tentative.

Shannon was just trying to think of what to say when Sheri returned. She entered Shannon's office with a flair and set a shopping bag on Shannon's desk. "Hi! Glad I caught you two."

"Um, what's in the bag, Sheri?" asked Shannon.

"Oh, you two have spent so much time eating in restaurants, I thought you'd love to have a home-cooked meal. So, I bought all the stuff so Shannon can cook you dinner at her place." Sheri had a large smile on her face. "I know she'd love to. So. Gotta run. Later." With that, Sheri twirled and left the office.

"So," Shannon started carefully, "we can put this in the fridge and go someplace for a good meal . . ."

"Or?"

"Or you can take your chances with my cooking. Which by the way, may be questionable at best."

"I see you're leaning toward something other than cooking – for which I don't blame you. It's like Sheri asked me to your place for dinner. Maybe you could volunteer her to give blood." He said it with a smile.

"No. Actually, I'd love to fix dinner for you at my place." *Did I actually say that? God! I've got to figure out – I mean, what's going on? And what's going on with me?*

"Uh, that sounds great, actually, if it is okay with you." *Please. Please stop sounding like a complete idiot.*

Twenty -five minutes later, they pulled into Shannon's drive. They walked to the door. Shannon dropped her keys. They almost bumped heads as both bent to reach for them. "Sorry," said Will. As he stood, he saw a patrol car pass on the street.

Shannon opened the door and they entered the house. Will carried the bag to the kitchen and set it on the counter. "Well, let's see what Sheri bought." Inside the bag were tuna steaks, rolls, a tossed salad, fresh green beans, and a two pieces of cheese cake. There was also a bottle of Viognier. From the bottom of the bag, Will pulled out a small bag of gourmet coffee.

"Huh," said Will. "Even coffee for the dessert. Hey! She even drew a smiley face on the coffee."

Shannon was sipping some water, which immediately spewed out of her mouth.

"You okay?"

"Uh, yeah. It's nothing. Just didn't expect coffee, too."

"It's just coffee."

"It's never just coffee," Shannon whispered. Then, so Will could hear, "Anyway, shouldn't be too hard, even I can steam green beans and sear tuna."

"Let me give you a hand."

"Why don't you pop the wine while I try to find what I need to steam the beans and cook the fish. The wine glasses are there," she said pointing to a cabinet.

Will got out two glasses, found a corkscrew, and opened the

wine. He poured a little into each glass and stood, holding both. Shannon turned around. "Oh. Thank you." They touched glasses and sipped the wine. "Not bad. But that's just a librarian's judgement."

Will looked at Shannon. "Actually, very, very nice." Then, "And, I like the wine, as well."

Shannon blushed. She'd pulled out a pot for steaming the beans and a grill for the fish. "Here, let me help." Will filled the pot with water and put it onto the stove to boil the water.

"Do you mind if I get out of my work clothes and into house clothes?"

"Please, go ahead. I'll try not to screw anything up or burn anything down while you're changing," he said with a smile.

Shannon went into her bedroom. She removed her work clothes and put on a pair of jeans – not too tight, not too loose – and a t-shirt. Soft, fuzzy socks and moccasins completed the outfit. She looked at herself in the full-length mirror she'd used for her annual 'inventory' earlier, and gave a quick spritz or two of perfume under her shirt. She turned and looked at her room. It was neat and clean, although she thought they wouldn't get into this room – at least tonight – if ever. Then, *please stop acting like this is the first date you've ever had. It's only dinner. But is it really more than just dinner? So much seems to be riding on it. Why?*

As she entered the kitchen, she saw Will had put the salads into bowls and put them on the table. He'd also placed the wine on the table and set the places. "I hope you don't mind. I went ahead and started setting up. We might have the salads first and then do the tuna and beans."

"Oh. No. Not at all. Thank you." She saw the table had been set perfectly – as if by Emily Post herself. *A far cry from Robert. He was SO clueless.* Shannon walked to one side of the table. Will followed her and held her chair. "You don't really need to . . ."

"It's my pleasure."

Again, heat filled Shannon's face and she knew her hands were trembling, if only a bit.

Will took his seat.

"So, could I ask you something?" said Shannon.

"Sure. Anything you want."

"Are you as nervous as I am?"

"Yeah. Why is that?"

"I don't know. Maybe it's the way Sheri kind of ..."

"Yeah. Besides. I have to admit. I really like you. Really. And I guess – I don't know. I feel like a teenager on his first date."

"Me too. I mean, I really like you and I was hoping you'd like me, too. I know you've been all over the world and I'm just this small-town girl, and ..."

"Doesn't matter where you're from. You're beautiful, intelligent, great to be around. You're perfect. I'm ..." Will searched for the right words.

She noticed there was a little sadness that crept into what he was saying. *Maybe he doesn't want to think about leaving.* There was that warm dreamy feeling again.

"Yeah. Me too. Or you too. I'm not sure anymore. I feel like such an idiot," she replied.

"Here's an idea. Instead of worrying about whatever, why don't we just concentrate on having a nice dinner and conversation. Just enjoy each other's time and company. No expectations or pressures."

"Deal." Shannon said it, but wasn't sure it took all the pressure off. Her face was still hot and her hands trembling. Then, there were those butterflies. *I hope we don't end up having sex tonight. I'm not sure I could handle it.*

For his part, Will wasn't doing much better. *Smooth. Real smooth. Better start studying the Bible. I'm going to end up as monk somewhere.* But in his heart, he knew he hadn't said what he really felt. He wanted nothing more than to put his arms around Shannon. And he wanted to tell her what he hadn't told anyone else in a long time.

They toasted again, then Shannon asked, "So tell me more

about your work. I could probably tell you about work at the library in two minutes."

Will talked about his travels and how he was assigned stories. Shannon imagined it would be a wonderful experience – one she would enjoy reading about.

He took the salad bowls to the kitchen and together they began cooking what had to be cooked.

"Sometimes, you get a cushy assignment. A friend of mine live on a vineyard for a month. He picked grapes and lived with the workers. Got a great story about that area's wine. Then, you might get one to investigate a crooked politician. You never know."

"Sounds fascinating."

"It can be. Sometimes it can be dull, too."

"Like delivering a check to a library?"

"Oh, I don't know. I work pretty hard – it's almost an obsession – an obsession I love. I think this trip was a form of forced down-time. But this has turned out to be a very interesting and enjoyable venture."

"I'll bet you say that to all the girls." Shannon regretted it as soon as she said it.

"If that's your way of asking if there are any other girls, the answer is no. There aren't any other girls."

Shannon started to apologize, "I . . ." but she was cut off when Will placed his lips on hers and put his arms around her waist. He pulled her close. He kissed her softly, slowly. Shannon wasn't sure how long. Her heart was racing and her knees started to buckle. The heat within her abdomen grew. She hoped it might consume her. The kiss ended, and he kissed her once more. Again, softly, but for only a second or two. Her breath was coming sharply, deeply, and rapidly. He ran his right hand along the side of her head and down the back of her neck, lifting her hair. The touch of his hand on her head and neck made all cares and worries dissolve. She almost collapsed.

"I've wanted to do that . . ."

Shannon said, "Good thing everything is off the heat. Well, the food, I mean." And they both laughed.

"Are you okay," he asked. "I didn't want to . . ."

Shannon cut him off with a soft kiss. "Well, you didn't, so yes, I'm a bit more than okay." The burning remained.

They finished their dinner. Will insisted on helping with the kitchen.

Afterward, Shannon asked, "Would you like to sit in the living room while we finish our wine?"

"Yes. Very much."

They sat on the couch. Will pulled Shannon to him and turned so that she would be lying on his chest. She pulled a blanket off the back of the couch and spread it over them. Then, she reached up and turned off the light. Shannon stayed wrapped in Will's arms until the sun rose the next morning.

Thirty-two

Shannon hopped out of Will's SUV in the parking lot of the library before he had a chance to get to her side to open the door.

"Thank you, but I don't need to have you go to the trouble of opening my door all the time."

"It isn't trouble. It's a pleasure. And, it shows the respect you are due."

"Well, thank you." She felt herself blush. "I'd better get inside. I'm a little late, and I'm sure Sheri will be eager to hear about the evening." Shannon avoided saying it was a date. Will took a step closer, and Shannon looked into his blue eyes. Her heart was pounding. The last thing she wanted to do was 'get inside.'.

Will kissed her softly. "Thank you for a great evening."

"Thank you. Without you it probably would have been television on the couch."

"I hope you didn't miss anything important on TV."

"No. It was perfect."

Shannon turned and walked to the door. Before she opened it, she could see the reflection in the glass of Will watching her. *God, I think I'm falling in love. This could be a disaster, but I don't care.*

She opened the door and Will's image disappeared. She walked across the lobby and up the stairs to the administrative level. As she entered her office, she could see Sheri at her desk out of the corner of her eye. Shannon took her time putting her things away and logging onto the network. She straightened papers and looked through a few files. When she thought she'd made Sheri suffer enough, she dialed her number and said, "You might as well come over here."

Sheri might have bluffed by saying she needed a few minutes to finish something before coming over, but she was dying to know what happened, and if she bluffed, Shannon might just disappear for an hour or so.

Sheri plopped into one of the chairs, holding a folder, making it look like work if Lucy happened to show up. "You're in earlier than I expected this morning. I would have gotten coffee, but I didn't know if you might have had your fill – get it? – last night – or maybe this morning. Too much coffee and it makes it hard to think about work."

"Are we really going to continue with the whole 'coffee' metaphor?"

"We don't have to. We could talk about girl parts and boy parts and how the parts met and how long it took and all kinds of other things."

"Fine. Coffee it is. There was no coffee last night and no coffee this morning. There. Happy?"

"No. Profoundly. That's really sad. You didn't fake a headache did you, you coward?"

"No. It wasn't like that at all. After he kissed me . . ."

"Whoa! Let's make that more of a chapter than a footnote."

"We were getting things ready – the gourmet coffee with the smiley face was a nice touch, by the way. I went to the bedroom to change. When I came out, he had the wine poured and the salads on the table. We ate and talked. As we were cooking the tuna and steaming the beans, he kissed me. Soft and slow. And, again. It was very nice. Made my heart kind of pound and my knees a little weak. When we finished dinner, we went to the couch. He sat and pulled me to him – well, I kind of helped. He wrapped his arms around me. We stayed that way all night."

"Okay, not too bad, but even I'm chomping at the bit. You could have kissed and morphed that into something much more interesting."

Shannon seemed lost and not hearing what Sheri was saying. "You know, it was the best 'after sex' I ever had, and we didn't even have sex." She seemed to snap out of it. "Anyway, it was a lovely evening, and I didn't need coffee."

"And Will? How do you think this lack of coffee affected him?"

"He seemed fine, thank you. He drove me to work and dropped me off."

"No lumps in the trousers, no bent over walking out the door, nothing got stuck under the steering wheel on the drive over?"

"You need a boyfriend - or maybe something soothing that vibrates."

"Got two – just in case I wear one out. It happens. Still, sad you didn't have coffee."

"I'm not sure I'm ready for coffee. Coffee does weird things. You don't sleep. You can't eat. You think about possibilities – impossibilities. You worry. You dream. He'll be gone in two weeks. Coffee will just make that really painful."

"Yeah, but you haven't had coffee lately, and I'm not sure Robert counts. He was weak coffee – if he was coffee at all. Will could be two really great weeks that you'd remember for the rest of your life. And, it could be more. Remember, 'tis better to have loved and lost ...'"

"Tennyson. I'm betting he never loved or he never loved and lost. Bastard. I'm giving up on poetry. Just makes you cry."

"Wow!"

"Can I trust you with a secret?"

Sheri leaned forward. "Secret? Sure. BFF. Partner in abstinence."

"I'm falling in love, dammit."

Thirty-three

Will pulled the SUV into the hotel parking lot. He'd watched as he drove to make sure he wasn't being followed. He parked as close to the hotel as he could. It would make it more difficult if Shannon's ex had some devious trick in mind. As he got out of the vehicle, he looked around casually. Except for getting shot, and Robert had already proven capable of that, he didn't really fear for himself. *The guy's a coward. He isn't afraid of stalking and threatening Shannon, but he'd run away in terror if he tried to confront me.* The thought of Robert taking shots at Shannon or throwing rocks through her window angered him. Logically he knew he would be gone in a week or two. Emotionally, he wanted to protect this woman he'd just met. He was trying to tell himself he was just being protective, but he also knew when he was lying to himself. He was having feelings for her. Real feelings. Deep feelings.

The parking lot was almost empty, and there were no vehicles that were the make and color of Robert's. Will doubted he had the means to own two cars. Will headed for the hotel entrance. He thought of Robert and how he was complicating Shannon's life. He shook his head to clear the thoughts. *It wouldn't be sad if he stepped in front of a moving bus.*

Will went to his room, showered, shaved, and dressed. Jeans, casual shoes, Madras shirt, and a faded blue crewneck sweater. He ran through a Tai Chi form, noting which muscles seemed a little sore from sleeping reclined on the couch last night. As he did so, a smile came to his lips. *Great night.*

He had breakfast in the hotel restaurant, then he headed to the paper. He wanted to check on the rest of the documentation and see what he could find. On the way to the paper, he stopped for coffee and doughnuts. He was begging favors and wanted to show his gratitude.

When he entered the office of the Northern Coloradoan, he was greeted warmly. Nothing cheers an office like free coffee and doughnuts.

"Well, welcome back," said Julius. "Staff seems to like you, as well. Of course, they're busy grazing on your treats. Come winter they should have a fine layer of fat to protect them from the cold."

"Well, everyone has been so nice, I thought I'd do a little something to show my appreciation."

"As you can see, it is well received. So, come back to look at the files again? I've got to warn you, it's addictive. I've looked through them so many times, and I still come up short."

"I'm hoping a fresh set of eyes might just see something that strikes a chord."

Will spent the next two hours looking through the documents that Julius had put together. There was something, but it was just out of his reach. *Whatever it is, it wasn't just a simple motorcycle jump gone wrong. There's something else . . .*

"How's it going?" It was Julius, holding a cup of coffee and one of the doughnuts he'd managed to save.

"There's something, but I just can't quite put my finger on it."

"You don't have to tell me. I've tried to stay away from it, but it keeps coming back to haunt me."

"So, tell me your recollections of this whole thing."

"Well, you know the story of the jump – well almost jump. Guy comes out of nowhere and puts together this two-hundred-foot jump in roughly a week, maybe two. He should have known everything he needed to know – ramp angle, speed, all that, from Evel Knievel's jumps. Yet he comes up short – in more ways than one and drops seventy-five feet onto rocks. His medical people . . ."

"His medical people?"

"Yeah. He didn't use folks from here. Somehow, he got a medical team from elsewhere. Why, is that important?"

"Maybe. Please continue."

"Anyway, they pull him out of the wreckage and up the cliff. They got him into an ambulance – again, arranged by him, and carted him off to someplace. Two days later, all bandaged up, they check him into the local hospital – well, skilled nursing facility – with their own doctor. Stayed two weeks and then, he was gone.

Six months later, he does the same basic jump – over in Utah. Only this time he makes it. Of course, the promotion for the second jump was better than the first. More ads, more people, sponsors. A lot more money."

"Whatever happened to the motorcycle?"

"Funny you should ask. They pulled it out of the canyon and when he got more famous – had an office and everything – he put it in a display case. Keeps it there 'to remind him of his roots.' Never even cleaned it up."

"And his other jumps?"

"He made maybe eight more over the next four years."

"None after that?"

"He went to Hawaii on vacation. He was over there for about a month. There were rumors that he'd been killed, but news footage of him getting off the airplane back on the mainland quashed those. About a week later he made a statement that from then on, he would concentrate on promoting other daredevil stunts. He wasn't going to do any more himself."

Will sat for five minutes without saying anything.

"You okay? Something come to mind?"

"Again, something is there. I feel close to it, but I can't quite put my finger on it. I appreciate the information. Can I look through old issues of the paper – say starting a year before the jump?"

"Sure. Archives are in the back. We've got paper and digital. Which do you prefer?"

"Actually, if I could look at the paper, I'd appreciate it."

Will looked through the papers. He was thankful it was a weekly; he only had to look through sixty or so. He perused each carefully, taking care to look through things that most people would just dismiss. At last, he'd thought he'd found something. He went back through papers from a month before and after. He waved his hand. Julius walked over.

"Find something?"

"Yeah. About six weeks before the jump, there was a carny in town. Remember anything about that?"

"Carny? They used to come through. Maybe once a year. Back then, the university was smaller, well, it was growing. Before that, it was a college. As the college grew and became a university, graduates stayed around. Went to grad school. When they'd finished that, some had put down roots. A few companies needing graduate-level employees opened. The population grew and, for lack of a better term, became more sophisticated. Fewer and fewer were interested in going to a carnival, and the carnies stopped coming in. Still find a place in smaller towns, places where entertainment is scarcer. Why?"

"Seems like a good place to find a motorcycle daredevil. One of the ads says something about the motorcycle 'sphere of death.' Any ideas?"

"That was one of those big spheres made out of wire or something. Anyway, you could see right through it. But somebody on a motorcycle would ride around inside, up, down, around. This one was advertised as having a young woman standing inside while the motorcycle roared all around her."

"And?"

"Never happened. Not sure why. I think the young woman may have been the girlfriend of the motorcyclist and they broke up. When she left, there wasn't anyone dumb enough to get into the ball with this guy riding around and missing her by inches. Oh, I get it. You think this is where the motorcyclist came from. Good call. Now all you have to do is find the carny and get one of those very private people to tell you about it."

Thirty-four

Will got a list of the small towns in the region that had newspapers. Then, he returned to the library and used the computer system to widen the area of his search. The result was a list of fifty small towns. He planned to call each one and check on any carnivals that were coming through. Shannon suggested that she and Sherri each take fifteen and they would call those in an effort to shorten the search.

"Aren't you afraid that Lucy will come in and find you doing non-university work?"

"Oh, this is time for Lucy's conference call. She has one every week day between 1 and 3 PM. They never run short."

"Never?"

"Silly." It was Sheri. "She locks herself in her office and has this 'conference call.' It only took us about a month to figure it out. She's addicted to a daytime talk show. The only way she'd come out of that office before 3 PM is if her TV went down. Then, she'd probably have to run home to 'check on something.' We're safe – until three."

Will was on number twelve on his list when Shannon stuck her head in the door and said, "I think I got it. I got one, anyway."

Will went to her office and put the phone on speaker. Shannon was at her desk. Will and Sheri were seated in the chairs.

"I was calling to check on whether or not you folks had a carnival there, either setting up, in progress, or getting ready to move on. My associate said you might be the place."

"Yes. Can I ask why you're checking?"

"Certainly. My name is Will Daniels. I work for International News Service. Here in town I've been sponsored by Julius Frank at the Northern Coloradoan. I can send my credentials if you like."

"Well, that won't be necessary, Mr. Daniels."

"Will, please."

"Okay, Will. We do have a carnival setting up today. They'll run through the weekend," Will checked. That was four days. "and move on Monday. What's the interest?"

"Background mostly. We're running down leads on something that happened a decade or so ago. Do you have any ads for the carnival? Any history in your town?"

"Well, I've been at the paper for twenty-five years and lived in North Platte for almost fifty. This carny has been coming here every year I've been here. They usually draw a decent crowd, or they wouldn't keep coming back."

"Did they ever have anything out of the ordinary – like a motorcycle act?"

The line was quiet for a minute or two. "You know, come to mention it, years ago they advertised an act with a motorcycle driving around the inside of a big ball. Supposed to have someone standing inside when the bike was roaring around and around. I remember because I thought that would be a newsworthy item. Turns out, they cancelled that. Disappointing."

"Okay. I appreciate the information, Mr.?"

"Johnson. Bob Johnson."

"Well, thank you."

Will hung up the phone. He looked at the clock. 2:43. All in good time.

"Looks like I'm headed to North Platte. Where the hell is North Platte?"

"East of here. In Nebraska. About two hundred and fifty miles – four and a half hours by car, even out here."

"I guess I'd better get on the road, then."

"Want some company?" It was Shannon. Sheri was trying to study the wood pattern in the desk.

"We'll probably have to stay overnight. I'm not sure of the sleeping arrangements."

"I'll take my chances. I don't get out to scenic North Platte as often as I'd like."

Will thought he heard a note of sarcasm in Shannon's voice.

Will and Shannon left the office together. Shannon looked back to see Sheri give her two thumbs up. Shannon just shook her head. She wasn't sure why she'd volunteered for the road trip.

"I'll need to stop at my place for a couple of things if we're looking at an overnight. You know, so I don't look like something out of monster film tomorrow."

"Good idea. I'll grab a couple of things from the hotel. And, I doubt you could look like you came out of a monster film even if you tried."

In forty-five minutes, they were headed East on Colorado Route 14. It would be 76 miles before they got to the interstate, and it didn't take long for Will to understand the sarcasm of Shannon's comment about scenic North Platte. The landscape was bleak.

"So, this is scenic eastern Colorado? Can I ask why you volunteered to come?"

"You've never driven out here before. I can't have you falling asleep and driving off the road. You'd probably wake up somewhere in Kansas, maybe Nebraska. Wouldn't do for us to call your boss and tell him we lost you. If you start dozing and need a relief, I'm here."

"Thank you. And, it's nice to have you along."

Shannon looked out the window at the amber waves of grain and smiled. Bleak as it was outside, it was rosy inside and she was happy to be here.

It was eight o'clock and dark when they arrived in North Platte. Will pulled in to a semi modern-looking motel that had the 'Vacancy' sign illuminated. He parked the SUV and came around to Shannon's side to open her door.

"I'm going to have to be retrained to open my own doors when you leave." She regretted saying it as soon as she had. The thought of Will leaving saddened her.

They walked to the office. The floor was covered with a beige industrial carpet. The walls were neutral, as was the counter and the pictures on the walls. It was the kind of place meant to be soothing and non-offensive, but by doing that, it was actually somewhat depressing.

"Good evening." The desk clerk's name was Brandon.

"Hi, Brandon. We'd like a couple of rooms."

"Well, right now, we've only got the one. A couple of guests decided to stay a day longer at the convention, and we try to accommodate."

Will started to turn to Shannon. She said, "It'll be fine."

Will was going to ask what convention was being held in North Platte that was so irresistible to the guests, but he was too tired from looking at miles and miles of nothing but miles and miles and didn't really care anyway.

"I guess that will do." He handed Brandon his credit card.

"Since we only have the one, I'll give you the room at our regular room price. This is a really great room. Usually goes for twice as much."

"Uh, thank you. We really appreciate it." Will saw the room charge was for seventy dollars.

They collected their things and walked to the room. It was on the second floor.

The room was actually very nice, if a bit dated. There was a king-size bed – one. Will looked at Shannon and shrugged.

"It's fine," she said.

There was orange carpeting and mass-produced art work on the walls. The table, chairs, and other items were out of the 1980s – early 90s at the latest.

"And, you don't have to worry about me taking advantage. After that drive, I'm too tired to do much of anything."

"Well," Shannon countered with a weak smile, "this could have been the night, because I'm too tired to put up a fight."

"Do you suppose they have sandwiches in the restaurant?"

"Not in the mood for chicken fried steak and sausage gravy?"

"For, for what?"

"I'll explain later. But in this part of the country you can get fried pretty much anything – including corn flakes."

Will went to the restaurant and returned with sandwiches and bottles of water. While he was gone, Shannon showered. Will saw she was wearing a long t-shirt for bed – one that came down to her knees. She looked younger than he knew she was, and he thought she looked adorable. And vulnerable. Feelings of protection resurfaced. Then, he started to think how she would feel snuggled next to him. He shook his head to clear the thoughts. The thoughts were still there, and he began to feel a tightness in his trousers.

They ate in silence, too tired to talk. Will showered and brushed his teeth. He wore a t-shirt and running shorts to bed. They crawled in to the bed on their respective sides and turned out the lights. They were asleep in seconds.

Thirty-five

Wakefulness came slowly to Will Daniels. He'd been dreaming. It was an old dream, one he hadn't had in years. He was flying – like superman; drifting over a beautiful landscape at tree-top level. He used to say that when he had that particular dream, he was so rested he wouldn't have to sleep for at least two days.

Lying on his back, he opened his eyes halfway. The popcorn ceiling of the motel room came into view, and he began to remember where he was. He felt something on him, and looked down to see red hair covering his chest. He remembered Shannon and sighed.

Shannon's arm was draped across his chest and held him. He smiled at the pale and freckled arm. He felt her chest against his side and her right leg over his. She was curled into him. The softness of her body against his excited and relaxed him at the same time. He could smell the fragrance of her hair and skin. He felt the softness of her body in his arms. She was breathing – slowly – and he realized how much he loved the feeling of this beautiful young woman next him.

Shannon made a small sound. Will thought the closest description would be that of a kitten dreaming. A tingle ran through his body and he knew it had nothing to do with physical desire. It was joy at being here, thankfulness for this moment, desire to put his arms around her and squeeze. Shannon started to move, her hand stroked his side. Will lifted his arm and began to caress Shannon's back. She made that dreaming kitten sound again and pulled closer.

"You keep that up and I may never leave," she said.

"Who said anything about wanting you to leave?"

"I thought you were supposed to be the strong one."

"Why?"

"That's just what I've been told, you know, by a lot of guys."

"Guys who wanted to impress you with their, for lack of a better term, masculinity?"

Anna Leigh

"Yeah."

"Didn't work, did it?" he asked.

"No. Everybody has their strengths and weaknesses. I wonder what yours are – weaknesses, that is."

"Right now, it would appear to be a beautiful red-haired woman draped across me."

Shannon stretched up to kiss Will. *What am I doing? I shouldn't be teasing him like this. So, why do I feel like . .*

Shannon moved her hand to Will's chest and began to caress him. She felt him tremble slightly. "You okay?"

"I'm feeling a little . . ."

"A little what?" She put on a faux innocent smile.

"First, I'm having a bit of trouble finding my words."

"Oooo. Is there a second?"

"I'm feeling a little warm. You're enjoying this, aren't you."

"More than you'll ever know." She continued to caress his chest, making sure to run her fingers lightly over his nipples. He trembled again.

"This isn't fair. I can't get to . . ."

"To what?" she asked demurely.

But she was cut short when he rolled so that she was on her back and he was next to her, his leg between hers. He started to nuzzle her neck, planting soft kisses as he did so. His hand was on her waist.

Now, she was the one who trembled. She opened her neck to him, inviting more kisses. Her hand on his chest continued to excite him. She felt a growing firmness between his legs pressing against her. It matched the dampness she knew was between her legs.

Their breath was heavier now. Their lips met, their mouths crushing against each other. Their mouths opened. Neither was going to stop.

The door opened – stopped only by the security chain.

126

"Housekeeping."

"Oh, god!"

Both of them jumped.

"Oh, I'm sorry," came a voice though the partially opened door. "I can come back in a few minutes."

The door closed, but the mood had been broken. He rolled onto his back, groaning as he exhaled.

"Worst timing in the world," said Shannon. After a minute, "If I were you, I wouldn't leave her a tip."

After a few minutes of recovery from the precipice, she stretched and kissed him softly. "There. I hope that's better. Not as nice as it might have been. But I don't usually check into motels with someone and, well . . ."

"I didn't think you did. I uh, just . . ."

"You know, you're adorable when you don't know what to say. But it would also seem this would be a good time to get out of bed. Why don't you go first?" Then, she put on a faux innocent smile. As he went into the bathroom, Shannon punched the pillow, then fell back into the bed with a sigh of exasperation.

Thirty-six

Breakfast was relatively quiet. Neither ate everything. Both Will and Shannon were lost in a sea of thoughts, emotions, joys, fears, and worries. *The only thing more unsettling than coffee,* thought Shannon, *is almost having coffee.*

The motel clerk gave them instructions to the area where they would find the carnival. The first show was going to be tonight.

"What are you going to do when we get there?" she asked.

"I'll see if there is anyone who has been with the carnival for the time when the accident happened. See if they remember someone from that time who might have left then made the jump."

It only took a few minutes to drive to the field where the carny was setting up. They pulled into a makeshift parking area. Tents, rides, games and concessions all seemed to be set up, waiting for the first of the patrons. Will got out of the SUV and walked to Shannon's side. She waited for him to open the door.

"Thank you," she said.

They walked toward what might be called the midway. A man in faded jeans and old long-sleeved shirt approached. "We don't open until five."

"Thanks," said Will with a smile. "We were looking for the manager."

"For?"

"We're doing some background on a story we're writing. We hoped the manager might be able to help us out."

"Trailer at the far end," he said, then turned and walked away.

"Friendly sort," said Shannon.

"Carnival folks tend to stick together and they're pretty protective of their turf. Strangers asking questions have never been known to bring good news or profit."

Eventually, they found their way to the trailer at the far end of the carnival. Will knocked on the door. No answer. He knocked again.

"If you're looking for Ben, he isn't here. Won't be back until just before we open." The voice was deep and powerful. Shannon turned to see a huge African American man. All muscle. His face showed no expression.

"Trying to find out about somebody who might have worked here – maybe ten years ago."

"Wouldn't be me."

Will looked at the man's arm. "Hundred and first?"

"Yeah. You?"

"Different, but worked with them from time to time."

They shook hands. "Daniels."

"Jenkins. Head that way. You'll want to talk to Bailey. Have to prove yourself. If you're bullshittin' he'll know."

As they walked, Shannon asked, "What was that all about?"

"Got my foot in the door, anyway. We're members of the same club."

"The – what?"

"Anybody who has served honorably in the military is part of a club. We feel it is exclusive. It means you have higher values."

"And?"

"And that seemed to do the trick. Now, we have to find Bailey, whoever that is, and convince him to talk."

"Is that what he meant by prove yourself?"

"Yeah. Wonder what the test will be."

They found Bailey in a field beyond the carnival. There were a few trees and large open area. Bailey was standing by a table. He was thin and looked weathered. There were guns on the table.

"Bailey?"

"Who wants to know?"

"Jenkins sent me over. Said you might be able to help me.

Daniels." They didn't shake hands, which Shannon thought a little weird. As before, she was almost ignored. Will seemed to have changed in his demeanor. Given the seeming foreign nature of these men, she was just as happy to be ignored.

"Why'd he send you?"

"Guess we had common friends in the past."

"Handle a shotgun?"

Bailey picked up a shotgun and loaded it. Will turned to her. "You might want to put your fingers in your ears."

Bailey picked up a small clay object, which she later found out was called a pigeon, threw it into the air, and when it started its descent, shot it. The pieces went splattering in all directions. Then, he handed the gun to Will and nodded to more clay targets on the table.

Will picked up one and threw it into the air. At the top of the arc, Will shot it as neatly as had Bailey. He handed the gun back.

Bailey reloaded the gun, picked up two clays and threw them. They separated and Bailey shot each. Again, he handed the gun to Will.

This continued until both men threw six and shot each. Will got his sixth just before it hit the ground.

"Not bad," said Bailey. "How are you with a pistol?"

Will smiled. "I do okay."

"Playing card on the tree." And he pointed to a tree about fifty feet away. "Sights are true."

Shannon could barely make out three small rectangles on the tree.

Will picked up a pistol from the table, loaded it, and held the pistol in two hands, straight out in front of him. Shannon heard the pistol bang eight times, each about two seconds apart. With each shot, the pistol pitched up, then Will sighted it again.

After the eight shots, Will removed the magazine and checked to see the gun was unloaded. They walked to the tree in silence. On the tree were three playing cards. One had a large irregular hole in the center. Bailey pulled it off. "Not bad."

"I'm a little rusty."

"Rifle?"

"Better."

"Why don't we get something to drink. And you can tell me what you want to know."

Thirty-seven

They walked to a small trailer. Bailey got three cokes. They sat in the shade.

"Ten years ago, or so, I think there may have been a guy with the carnival who rode motorcycles – as part of an act. Then, I think he left the carnival to strike out on his own. I was hoping somebody might remember him and a name. Had an act where he was going to ride around in some metal ball."

Bailey thought for a few minutes. He took a pack of cigarettes out of his pocket, and lit one. Halfway through the cigarette he said, "Yeah, actually there was. He was supposed to ride his bike around the inside of this giant ball. Girlfriend was going to stand inside. I don't think she had any idea. After their first practice, she took off. Pretty little thing. Hope she married somebody better than him. Name was – Taggart. No. Tanner. No. Tasker. Yeah. Tasker. Riley Tasker. When there wasn't any danger of some girl getting hurt, you know, to pull a better crowd, Ben cancelled the act – got money back on that stupid ball – and made Tasker a roustabout."

Will was elated. He finally had a name, if it was the guys real name, and the right guy. He started to thank Bailey, but he continued.

"Two other guys used to hang out with this guy. They were pretty useless. No real act. Not strong enough to be roustabouts. Always had a plan, though. Twins, or close enough to look like it. They left about the same time. Good riddance. Russell was the last name. Don't remember anything else."

"I appreciate it. This may be a big lead. Can't thank you enough. Let me know if I can do anything for you."

Bailey walked over and shook Will's hand. "Proud to serve." Will looked at him and said, "Proud to serve."

Will and Shannon walked back to the SUV in silence. Will opened Shannon's door and helped her in – almost as if in a trance. He walked to his side and got in.

"Okay. We've got three people. One guy who is apparently

pretty good on a motorcycle and two more. All left about the same time. I wonder if they could have put together the idea for the jump."

"Yes, we've got names, but it's like having the name John Smith. It doesn't really bring us closer to who they really are."

"Well, we'll hang out in beautiful metropolitan North Platte until before the carny opens and see if the manager can help us out. Sad thing is, I'm not sure carnivals keep really good records."

They lunched in a diner and spent a little time wandering the shops. Everyone was offering carnival specials. About four thirty, they headed back to the carnival. Ben was in his office. He wasn't in the mood to provide any information until Will mentioned that Bailey had given him names of workers.

"Bailey?"

"Yeah, why?"

"Bailey doesn't talk to anyone. How'd you get him to open up?"

"We did a little shooting."

"You must be damn good if he talked to you afterward."

"I did okay."

"I'll give you this on the strength that Bailey actually talked to you."

Ben opened a file drawer. It took about five minutes before he pulled out a ragged folder and paged through the contents. He grabbed a pad on his desk and wrote out the information. "Tasker – Riley Tasker, from Fremont, kind of northwest of Omaha. The Russell boys, Sam and Phil – Council Bluffs. That would be like an eastern suburb of Omaha. Those are the addresses and – I shouldn't give this to you," he handed Will a copy of their employment files. "Photo that, if you want. I need the original. Like Bailey said, Tasker was pretty good on a motorcycle. But half his act left. The other two, well, I was getting ready to fire them when they left."

Will used his phone to photograph the pages. He thanked the manager and they walked back across the field to the SUV. Excited carnival patrons were starting to arrive as they pulled onto the street. He stopped at a convenience store to get a few things for the trip back. Then, he stopped for gas.

"We're going to be driving back in the dark," said Shannon.

"Yeah. I know. I drove out. Remember? The way I see it, it will be better to go back at night and not see the nothing that wasn't here when we drove out."

Shannon laughed. She tilted her seat back and before long the smooth road and rocking vehicle put her to sleep.

Thirty-eight

"Okay," started Sheri after Shannon had related the highlights of her trip, "so you've figured out how to throw cold soda on his – you know – and now, it seems you figured out how to rub the magic lantern and make it come close to exploding. There are other uses, just sayin.'"

"It wasn't like that. I woke up. We apparently 'found' each other over the course of the night. I kissed him and my hand wandered. Then, we just kind of – you know. It was just spur of the moment."

"It could have been a spurt of the moment. Damn housekeeping."

"Did your brain stop developing in eighth grade?"

"This is serious stuff. My best friend is on the verge, you know. We've got to find a way to get you past the, uh, verge."

"Yeah. I'm not sure just what's going to happen, although the natural progression would seem to be . . ."

Will walked through the door. He had a bag in his hand. "Morning ladies. Ready for a pick-me-up I trust."

"Oh god!" said Sheri. "You've got to tell me where you get these things. They're the best I've ever had. You can't be making them in your hotel room. And no place around here makes anything this good. Ooooo! Cherry." She eyed Shannon.

"You're going to make me fat," said Shannon, picking up the cheese Danish and taking a bite.

"I doubt it. Wouldn't matter, though, you'd still be beautiful." With that, he leaned over and kissed her. Sheri stared wide-eyed.

Will turned to set the bag down. When he did, Shannon stuck her tongue out at Sheri, who returned the favor.

"Just to show you I'm not just another pretty face," said Shannon, "I heard the strangest thing on the radio coming in to work this morning. I thought it would be of interest."

"There were these twins – Tonia and Becky – identical twins.

Nobody could tell them apart. When they were growing up, they got frustrated when people couldn't keep them straight. Then, they came up with a plan. Becky was good at math. Tonia was good at languages. So, they'd dress the same and Becky would go to her math class and Tonia's. Especially on test day. Tonia would do the same for languages. Some days, they'd even wear different outfits ad switch during the day."

"Um, go on," said Will.

"Well, they apparently had so much fun doing this they started swapping roles in all kinds of things. When they were teenagers, they even swapped boyfriends on occasion. Apparently, one was a better lover than the other – just a rumor - still. Anyway, they got married. But they couldn't resist. So, on occasion, they swapped husbands, as well."

"Holy..."

"Yes. And, one of them got pregnant – by the other's spouse. So, the other one, with some difficulty, did the same. They actually lived with the other husbands until the babies were born. Then switched back to their original spouse. Nobody ever knew. Well, now they do."

"Holy crap!" It was Sheri.

Will was staring, lost in thought.

"So, these two families actually have mixed children – some from the wife, and some from the sister. I mean, the mind boggles. It's like some bizarre comedy that hasn't quite blown up yet. They always do, you know. Something always goes wrong. Just thought it might be of some interest – you know."

Will got up and walked to Shannon. "Yes. It is. Now, all we have to do is prove it." Then, he kissed her full on the lips.

Thirty-nine

Will sat in Frank Julius' office. He had a small stack of eight by ten black and white photographs and held a magnifying glass in his hand. He scanned each photograph carefully, paying special attention to areas that wouldn't usually be noticed.

"Find something?" It was Frank.

"Not yet. It's like trying to come up with a word or a name. It's right on the tip of your tongue, but you can't quite put your finger on it. I know, that's mixing metaphors. But you get the idea."

"Well, I tried to find out about social security numbers on our motorcycle friend, but he's a private individual. Doesn't have to reveal any of that. Plus, he's paid through a private corporation. His own. You'd have to have a court order to look at that stuff. Sorry."

"No problem. I have an idea who they are. Now, I just have to figure out why they did what they did. I may know the how."

"Care to share?"

"Not until I'm sure. But when I am, you'll be the first to know." Will returned to the photographs. A half hour later he said, "There you are. Gotcha now you son of a . . ."

Will put the photographs away after making a copy of the last one he looked at. He left the office feeling elated. *Almost there. Almost there.*

He walked to his SUV. *Not ready to share with everyone, but I'll run it by Shannon. See what she thinks. Maybe she can add something. Close. So very close.*

Forty

Will arrived at the library at 3 PM. Shannon was stuffing papers into her bag.

"What's up?"

"Oh, glad you're here. I was going to call. There's a faculty/staff mixer of sorts – they call it something else, like it is an important event. Anyway, Lucy decided it would be nice to go – and drag you along. I guess she wants to show you off."

Will just stared.

"I'm going to run home and get into something else. This is where we'll be – upstairs in the student union." Shannon had a diagram of the student union and pointed out where the room was. "It will take me awhile to change – well, not too long, but you know how it is with ladies. I'll meet you there in an hour. Okay?"

"Yeah. Sure." Although Will wasn't quite sure about anything. "Do I need to . . ."

"Well, I hate to make you run to your hotel, but I'm sure Lucy would appreciate a sport coat."

"Okay. An hour? There?"

"How about we meet in the lobby of the student union. I'm sure Lucy would love to introduce you to everyone, but it might be better if I were there to run interference."

"Yeah. Sure."

Fifty minutes later, Will was in the lobby of the student center. Surrounded by students wearing jeans, shorts, and t-shirts, he felt out of place in gray dress slacks, a blue blazer, white shirt, and solid red bow tie. He felt conspicuous, and he didn't like being conspicuous. He heard the click of a woman's heels on the terrazzo floor. He turned to see Shannon walking toward him.

She was wearing a knee length royal blue sleeveless sheath dress. Her three-inch open toe heels and clutch were white. A small diamond pendent and diamond earrings provided sparkle. Her red hair and pale skin only magnified the effect. She walked up to Will and said, "So?"

"Okay?! I'm surprised my mouth didn't drop open. You're absolutely gorgeous. Not that you aren't anyway, but . . ."

"Kind of makes you want to drool, doesn't she?" It was Sheri, walking up. She was wearing a cranberry sheath. Her shoes and purse were cream colored.

Will blushed.

"We'd better get this over with."

Shannon walked to the staircase leading up to the meeting room. When she reached the first stair, she turned and looked at Will. His eyes were locked on her. What she saw in them was admiration mixed with – with something that made her tingle.

"Coming?" she asked, then turned red when she realized the double entendre she hadn't meant.

He and Sheri joined her and they climbed the stairs and entered the room, Will with a woman on each arm. Lucy, wearing a little black dress, came over studying Shannon with each step.

"Why Shannon, you look . . ."

"Thank you, Lucy. As do you."

"Well, we should introduce Mr., uh, Will, around." With that she turned and started scanning the room.

Sheri leaned toward Shannon and whispered, "This is why I hate going places with you. It's like being the moon – standing next to the sun."

"You look beautiful, as well. You know that."

"Not that anybody noticed."

Will had been concerned that he would be underdressed, but saw that most of the women were dressed much better than the men, who looked like their Sunday best was a tweed sport coat and dockers.

Lucy brought over the first of a long line of people she wanted to impress with what she referred to as "my donor." Will lost track after the first two. He was mesmerized by Shannon. At the moment, she was talking with a man and woman. She had a champagne flute in her hand. Will thought she looked like royalty.

After ninety minutes, Will was seeking refuge by a large window that overlooked an open area behind the student union. He was silently praying he wouldn't be found.

A voice came from behind him. "Excuse me, sir. Are you the famous donor that Lucy Crandall has been introducing to the faculty and staff?"

Will turned, with his best false pleasant face plastered on. It was Shannon, champagne flute in hand, smiling.

"Thank god! I am SO glad it is you. I'm not sure I can take any more of – this," he said, gesturing to the large group in the room.

"Me either – or neither. Whichever. Anyway, I guess I didn't eat lunch, and the champagne seems to have hit me harder than I realized. Sheri drove me over, but I don't want to ruin her good time. I hate to drag you away, but could I impose upon you to take me home?"

"For so many reasons, I would be thrilled to get you home safe and sound. Let me figure out what to tell Lucy."

"Try not to say your girlfriend got trashed and you have to get her home before she passes out." Then, she giggled. Will smiled. *Girlfriend.*

He found Lucy and made some excuse about not feeling well. He hoped he didn't upset her. For her part, Lucy was gracious. She'd already introduced him to everyone she wanted to. She only planned to stay a few minutes longer herself.

Forty-one

The ride to Shannon's only took a few minutes. Will pulled the silver SUV into the drive behind Shannon's car. He removed his sport coat and tie as he exited the vehicle and went to Shannon's side. He held the door and steadied Shannon as she left the vehicle. He walked her to the door. Shannon dropped her keys.

"Oops."

"You'd better let me get these. Wouldn't want you going head-first off the porch and into the shrubs."

"That's very gentlemanly."

Will opened the door and they stepped inside. Shannon kicked off her shoes, immediately dropping three inches in height. Will slipped out of his shoes. He didn't want to take the chance of stepping on her feet by accident.

"This way," she said, turning and heading for the bedroom.

Will followed her. She was standing next to her bed. Her work clothes were on the foot of the bed.

"Uh do you have a t-shirt, or something I can get for you?" he asked, turning to look for a closet or dresser. Just as he spotted the dresser, he heard the sound of a zipper. As he turned, he saw Shannon's blue dress slide down her body and land at her feet. She bent down, picked it up and set it on the foot of the bed, together with her work clothes. The only thing left on her body was a very sheer bikini brief, which covered nothing and gave new meaning to the term brief.

"So?"

"Uh, we need to get you into something. T-shirt? Something?"

"That mirror," she said pointing to a full-length mirror in the corner. "That's what I use every six months or so. Try to figure out if I'm falling apart. I'd ask you, but you've never seen me without clothes, so you don't have any reference. I suppose I could have you look at me naked twice a year and give me your opinion. I know I'm talking too much, but I'm feeling a little nervous."

Will looked at her. She was beautiful. Almost beyond words.

Her figure was perfect. She seemed tiny, delicate. He stood in awe. He realized he was feeling love, reverence, but most of all, he was feeling protective. He didn't want anything to hurt this beautiful woman.

"So? You didn't turn and run. That's a plus."

Shannon's words shocked Will out of his reverie. He took a step toward her, "No, it's ..."

His words were cut off. She stepped to him, put her arms around his neck, and kissed him passionately on the lips. He reacted by putting his hands on her back and pulling her toward him.

"Wait. No."

"Why?" She asked as she looked at him.

"This may sound stupid – maybe even to me right now, but I happen to believe it's wrong to take advantage of a lady – woman – when she's had too much to drink and might do something she otherwise wouldn't." *Regret in the morning,* he thought.

"Well I can tell you're not from around here. All the guys I've known seem to live by the creed, get 'em drunk as fast as you can then jump on them before they can fight you off. Then, they can get on with the important stuff in their lives, you know, pool, drag racing, bar fights."

"Yeah. Well, I don't work that way. It isn't civilized. I'm not sure it's human. So, I don't ..."

He was cut off by another kiss.

"Just so you know. I only had the one glass of champagne. I'm not drunk. And I'm also not sure I'm not the one taking advantage. So, to be sure, if you'll remove what's left of my clothing, I'll assume you're not acting under duress."

She felt Will's fingers slide from her back to her hips, then under the waistband of the briefs. She felt him slide them slowly to the floor, taking his time, caressing her legs as he did so. He was on his knees, sliding the briefs from one foot, then the other. Shannon complied, then felt a soft kiss on her tummy, just under her navel. Her heart sped. Her knees weakened. *Ooooooooo. You can do that all night.*

Will lifted her and carried her to the bed. Then, he pulled off his shirt. Shannon ran her hands over his chest and back. They kissed. Their lips met. Shannon ran her tongue across his lips, then pushed into his mouth. He pulled back then began kissing her neck. She turned her head to open herself more completely. Soft kisses rained on her neck, then her shoulders. Kisses like the lapping of soft waves. Hands massaging softly. She was lost in a dream, laying in the surf, feeling the lapping of the water, knowing it was him all along. Soft kisses caressed her breasts, making her breathe deeply. Soft kisses on her tummy, almost tickling, but softly massaging. Lower he kissed. Lower and closer, until – there! She sucked in her breath as she felt him touch her – YES! THERE! Oh! Nobody had ever . . . It was exquisite. Relaxing, energizing, teasing. Lips and tongue, caressing, sucking, probing. It was the ocean caressing her with waves. Only these waves were pulsing, tingling, pushing, electric. Energy was building. Her heels dug at the sheets. She was aware of her legs moving, pushing, knees opening and closing. She was twitching, moving. The waves continued, stronger. Nothing was. . . Was what? *Oooooo!* Power surged. A wave exploded from her core out to her fingers and toes, then back. She felt her whole body tighten. She was standing on a water fall. A jolt ran through her body. Energy poured through and around her. She was shaking uncontrollably. She floated off the waterfall and dove into a pool of complete satisfaction, relaxation and safety. She lay immersed in what she thought heaven must feel like.

Slowly, Shannon came back to reality. It began with an awareness that she was being kissed and massaged on her legs. *If this continues, I may never get out of bed again.* Soft kisses followed softly massaging hands. Thighs, knees, calves, then feet. *Nobody has ever . . .* The kisses returned to her knees, then thighs. He was getting close to . . . *Ooooo! Woooow!* Shannon tensed as he touched her there, yes THERE, again. She was afraid she would be so sensitive she would jump out of bed. But the kisses were soft. He was licking. Probing. She felt his tongue push into her. *Oh my god! You can't - not twice. Maybe. Oooooo!* Her heels were digging into the bed again. Her hands pulled the sheets. The waves returned – strong and powerful. Pushing and pulling. She felt him kissing her stomach and wanted to tell him not to stop. He worked his way to her breasts, then neck.

"I don't have ...," he whispered.

She reached for her night stand and pulled the drawer. Her hand digging into the contents. Frantically. After what seemed like an eternity, she pulled out an unopened package of three condoms.

"A gift from Sheri," she said hoarsely. "A lifetime supply. I didn't think I'd ever ..."

She was cut off by his mouth on hers. They kissed with their mouths open lips sliding across one another in the wetness. Their tongues were dancing, exploring. She heard the box rip open, then one of the packages. His lips were on her neck. Then, she felt him touch her, his hardness pushing slightly within her. A slight withdrawal. Then a deeper push. *Oh god! He's teasing me!* All she knew and felt was she wanted all of him. She wanted to consume him. She pulled. Deeper he plunged. Finally, she put her hands under his bottom and pulled. He pushed and filled her completely. It was almost too much. Almost. Then, they moved together. She felt his stomach on hers, his chest against her breasts. His hips were between her legs. She lifted and spread her thighs. He pushed deeper. Her ocean now a tempest. She was being pushed and pulled. His head was nuzzled in her neck. She felt his deep, forceful breath on her chest and breasts. His stubble scratching her skin. She pulled his head to her. All her limbs tightened and pulled inward as she exploded again, and dropped into her pool of bliss.

Forty-two

It was dark when Shannon opened her eyes. She and Will were still naked. She was curled in his arms. He was breathing softly and slowly. He seemed to be in a deep sleep and she wondered if he always slept this well.

She slipped out of bed and into the bathroom. She wanted to see how much damage all the physical activity had done. Surprisingly, she looked pretty good – considering. She felt pretty good, too. Okay, wobbly legs and a feeling that she had been completely drained, but that was to be expected. As she looked at herself in the mirror, she saw a woman completely in love. Satisfied and happy, too. A soft glow emanated from within. A smile on her face. She returned to bed, curling herself once again in Will's arms, feeling safe and in love.

"Everything okay?"

"Yes. Probably perfect. I thought you were asleep."

"I sleep well, even when it's noisy, but wake when something 'different' happens. Like when the beautiful sensuous woman I'm lying next to gets out of bed."

"Most guys around here don't care about much once they're done. If you get my drift."

"Those guys don't know what a precious gift it is to be in your presence."

Shannon kissed his arm and snuggle against him. She felt his hand on her stomach. He started to massage her – softly, so very softly. She felt him starting to grow behind her. "Three times? In one night? This is like my quota for the decade." Then, she turned and kissed him.

Forty minutes later, they lay panting and sweating. "Well, if you count satisfaction, this may be my quota for the century." Will kissed her. Then, he put his arms around her, and pulled her close. Shannon stated making figure eights on his chest with her finger. She sighed deeply, and for no particular reason, kissed his nipple. Will jumped. "Oh, my! Somebody is sensitive."

"Just remember," he said, "this one was entirely you fault."

"Again?! Wait, I'm not sure. I mean . . . Oh, what the hell."

A full hour later, they lay on their backs, completely spent.

"Truce," said Will.

"Truce," responded Shannon. "I hope I'll be able to walk in the morning. And, I know Sheri is going to say something. I know I'm going to have that freshly fu . . ., let's make that freshly satisfied look on my face. Maybe I can take a week's vacation. Oh! I know Sheri. When she asks, and she will, if you got in okay – wink, wink, nudge, nudge, PLEASE don't laugh, don't giggle, and don't quickly try to count either the fibers in the carpet or the tiles on the ceiling. Just thank her for her concern about your welfare."

"That bad?"

"You have no idea. This will be THE topic of conversation for the entire school year. She may take out a Will board."

"Got it. Just lie about the most wonderful night of my life."

They dozed off and woke tangled in each other when the sun rose. He kissed her softly, almost delicately.

"I love you."

Shannon diverted her eyes. "That isn't going to make it any easier when you have to leave. You're not the one standing at the airport after the plane leaves – tears on her cheeks and red eyes."

Will put his arms around Shannon and kissed the top of her head. "It's not going to be any easier for the one on the plane. I could have just kept my mouth shut, and maybe I should have. It is important to me for you to know how I feel."

"Then you might as well know that I have fallen in love with you, too." They kissed again. "Now, you'd better get to the bathroom.

Will kissed Shannon, showered quickly, dressed and left for his hotel. Shannon crawled out of bed twenty minutes later hoping a hot shower would ease some of the soreness she felt.

She looked at herself in the mirror. After all the activity, she was surprised there wasn't any bruising, although they hadn't really done anything that would have drawn a bruise. *Just good old exhaustive, passionate, mind-bending sex.* She saw the face of a woman in love, a woman satisfied. A woman with a feeling of excitement, passion, and calm within her. And, if it didn't last, it didn't matter – not this morning anyway. Maybe Tennyson was right. It would be better not to find out.

Forty-three

Will pulled into the library parking lot mid-morning. He grabbed the bag of Danish and headed to Shannon's office. Shannon wasn't in, but Sheri popped out of her office when she saw him. She had a devilish look on her face.

"Before we get to the main event," she said, "I'm hoping you included me in your Danish run this morning."

Will opened the bag. Sheri practically stuffed her face into the bag. "Oooooo. Which one? Which one?"

Will moved the bag and lifted out a wrapped pastry.

"Oh. Cherry. My favorite." She unwrapped it halfway and took a healthy bite. "You don't have to play coy. She's been in and I pumped her for information. She folded like a cheap TV tray. I know it all. So..."

"So, I guess you don't need anything from me."

"I just want to hear your version."

"Did you get that technique from a cop show? 'Your accomplice already told us everything. If you have something to say in your defense, you'd better tell us now.' Really?"

"Can't blame a girl for trying. Before she left, she had this look I've never seen before. Worn out, completely relaxed, ecstatically happy. I swear she was humming."

"Humming?"

"Humming. You responsible for that?"

"Maybe she's just happy. Beautiful morning."

"My guess is it was a beautiful night, as well."

Sheri returned to her office. Will sat in Shannon's office reviewing the information he'd collected. Just before noon, Shannon's phone rang. When there wasn't any answer, Sheri's phone rang. Sheri motioned to Will.

When he entered Sheri's office, she said, "She got a call from Lucy's assistant before you got here. She'd gotten a call from admin and Shannon had to go over and sign some paperwork.

That was Lucy's assistant. She wanted to know why Shannon hadn't gone to admin yet."

"Where's the administrative building?"

"It's over next to – never mind. I'll walk over with you." Sheri picked up her purse and motioned down the hallway.

Sheri turned down a small corridor, went through a nondescript door, and started down a stairway. The steps and walls were concrete. Their footfalls echoed in the stairwell. "Okay, I said I wasn't going to beg, but I need to know where you get those Danish. And, whether the recipe would make me fail a drug test."

Will seemed distracted. "Huh? Yeah. Later."

They exited the building in a narrow area between the library and another building. There was a small patch of grass between the building and sidewalk. Will stopped in his tracks.

"What . . ?" started Sheri. She looked at where Will was staring. On the grass was an opened purse. The contents were scattered.

Will walked over and picked something up. When he turned, Sheri saw it was pepper spray cannister. "Empty," he said. "He ambushed her out here."

"Robert?"

"Yes. Robert. I should have known and checked earlier. We've got to find her." Will was looking around as if he might see her or them.

"You don't think he'd actually hurt her?"

"I don't know what he might do. He's crazy with jealousy. He thinks he owns her. If she resists . . ."

"Wait!" Sheri was digging in her purse. She pulled out her phone and started punching the display.

"What are you . . ?"

"Shush!"

Will was quiet while Sherri completed what she was doing. "There. Thank god!"

"What?"

"We've got an app. It's called 'Find My Friends.' Her phone is on, so I can get her location on my phone."

Will grabbed her and kissed her on the forehead. "Okay. Where is she?"

"Looks like they are headed out of town. Here. See?"

"Let's go!"

"Where?"

"We're going to follow them."

"Wait!" Sheri ran to the corner of the building and came back. "They didn't take her car. She must be in his."

Will and Sheri ran to his SUV. He opened the door for her then ran to his side and jumped in. "Call the police. Tell them that we strongly believe Shannon has been kidnapped by her ex-boyfriend, uh, Robert . . ."

"Barr."

"Yeah, Barr. Anyway, he's got her in his car and we're following using your app. Tell them where they are now and what direction it looks like they are going. Let's hope the app holds and the signal doesn't fade. Oh, yeah. Ask If they can let Sargent Jack Hawkins know." Will handed Sheri his phone so she could keep the tracking app open.

"Hi!" he heard Sheri begin, "My name is Sheri Chapman. I believe a co-worker – and friend – has been kidnapped."

Two minutes later she had given them all the information she could. The dispatcher cautioned them not to follow the suspected felon. Will just laughed. "Right. Why don't we just pull off and get a soda or something while we wait to see what happens?"

Sheri looked worried. They were on a two-lane road. The speed limit was forty-five. Sheri knew because she caught the sign as a blur when they passed it doing ninety.

"Looks like they're headed for Snakebite Canyon," he heard her say. She was studying the display. She repeated the information for the policeman on the other phone. She felt a bit of relief when their speed dropped to sixty, but she saw why. In a gravel parking area ahead was Robert's blue sedan. The car appeared to be empty.

"Are they here?"

"No. It looks like they're over there – up one of the trails."

"This place doesn't have any trails," said Will as he pulled to a stop. He got out of the SUV and went to Sheri's side and opened her door.

"Okay. You stay here. When the police come, point them in the direction where you see Shannon."

"You shouldn't . . . What are you planning to do?"

"Whatever I can. Maybe it will only be a distraction, but I need to do whatever it takes."

Will headed off quickly but carefully in the direction Sheri had indicated. She wasn't sure what to do. She didn't want to just stand there, but she knew Will shouldn't try to stop Robert. She hoped the police would arrive soon.

Will was crouched, moving from one rock outcropping to the next. After he'd gone about a hundred yards, he heard the faint sound of voices in the distance. He redoubled his caution. He didn't want Robert to see him before he was ready. Finally, he could see the two of them. They were about thirty feet away. Rocks, brush, and other obstacles would make a direct run at Robert an impossibility. Robert had a knife. He was walking around Shannon who was seated on a rock. He was gesticulating wildly, the knife flashing in the sun.

"Dammit Shannon. You're going to have to get in line. I'm going to have to tie you up or something until you realize your place. Your place is with me. You don't seem to get that."

"Robert," started Shannon quietly, "it's over. It has been. I'm not yours and my place is where I want it to be."

"Stop saying that! I'll tell you where you're supposed to be! I'll tell you!"

Will took a deep breath, not sure if he was ready for this and stepped into the open. "Hello Robert."

Forty-four

An unmarked black SUV braked and pulled into the lot. The tires crunched in the gravel. When the vehicle stopped, all four doors opened. Three police officers exited. First, out of the passenger side, was a stocky, good-looking man. He had three yellow chevrons on his sleeve. His nametag read Hawkins. Two officers got out of the back. One had two yellow chevrons on his arm. Those two officers went to the back of the SUV. Sergeant Hawkins strode up to Sheri.

"Chapman?"

"Yes. Yes."

"I'm Hawkins. You know where they are?"

Sheri showed him her phone, using her hand to block the sun from the screen. "There. That way, a hundred yards or so. I think."

The two junior officers walked up. They were wearing vests and had microphones on a headset. Each also had a military-style rifle. The man with two chevrons, Sheri saw his name was Jenkins, handed Sergeant Hawkins what looked like a hunting rifle. It had a telescopic scope on it.

Sheri was about to say something when Sergeant Hawkins said, "About a hundred yards that way. Jenkins right. You'll be two clicks. I'll be one. Johnson, take the left. You're three clicks. Let me know when you're in position. We'll try to flank him. I'll try to find a perch." He looked at Sheri and said, "You. Stay here. George!" The fourth officer got out of the SUV, a microphone in his hand. Hawkins pointed to Sheri. The man he called George nodded.

They started out in the direction Sheri had given them, slightly crouched, fanning out as they went. A hundred yards later, there were voices. Hawkins used hand signals to direct his men. A large outcropping was in front of him. He decided to climb it and look for the perpetrator. The sun was past its highest point. That meant it would be slightly at his back and slightly in Barr's eyes.

He topped the rocks and eased the rifle into a position of support. He popped the end caps on the telescopic scope and pointed the rifle at Robert. With the scope, it made Robert seem only a few feet away. He was gesticulating wildly, holding Shannon in front of him, waving a large hunting knife at her and at Will Daniels. He cycled the bolt, putting a live cartridge into the chamber. The rifle was made for hunting large game. If a bullet hit Robert anywhere, it would tear him apart. The problem was, Robert was hiding behind Shannon. To hit him would mean missing her by an inch or two. Soon, he received two clicks, then three on his headset – confirmation that everybody was in place.

Robert was yelling at Will. "You. It's all your fault. If you had just gone home and not caused any trouble, we wouldn't be here."

"Okay, it's all my fault. I admit it. I should have left. But I'm the one you hate. I'm the one you need to punish. Why don't you let Shannon go and we can do this? I don't have any weapons."

"You'd like that wouldn't you? As long as I've got her, you'll pretty much do whatever I want. I could even have you walk up here and slit your throat. You like that idea Mr. Bigshot?"

"Whatever you want. You're in charge. Just don't hurt Shannon. Let her go."

"Maybe after I've dealt with you."

Will took a step in Robert's direction."

"Wait! Stop! You stay there – for now."

Robert was getting more and more agitated.

There was a sound, something, off to the left – Robert's right. Robert turned his head to look, his knife pushing out in that direction. Shannon looked at Will. Will's right foot was braced against a rock. He started to push forward. As he did, he nodded to Shannon. She bent at the waist, then, straightened up. Will saw her more than straighten. She was using all her force to smash the back of her head into Robert's face.

Robert howled and dropped the knife. Shannon turned slightly and pulled her right foot to Robert's knee. She ran the side of her shoe down his shin and slammed the heel of her shoe into the top of his foot. He released his grip on her and as he did so, Shannon slid her hips to the left and raised her right fist above her head before she slammed it down and into Robert's crotch. Robert dropped to the ground rolling around, not knowing what to grab first, and howling in pain.

Shannon ran. When she was about ten feet from Robert, a policeman stepped from behind an outcropping. He beckoned her with his left arm, a military-style rifle in his right. "Here. Here." She ran to him and he guided her behind his back. Then he turned and aimed his rifle at a writhing Robert. When he did, a green laser dot joined a red one dancing on Robert's chest.

The officers approached and handcuffed Robert without any difficulty. "That bitch!" he yelled.

"I'd be careful what you say. Come along peacefully or we'll turn that little lady who just beat the tar out of you loose again."

Jack Hawkins shook his head; *I wonder if she'd like to be a cop. Dumb SOB had no idea what he'd gotten himself in for. Probably have been better off if we'd just shot him.*

Forty-five

The police were busy pulling Robert off the ground. Shannon heard the officer with two stripes begin, "Robert Barr, you are under arrest for the crimes of kidnapping, unlawful imprisonment, assault with a deadly weapon, and threats of violence. You have the right to remain silent. If you give up this right . . ."

Will and Shannon were running toward each other. Shannon wrapped her arms around Will's waist. Will wrapped his arms around her back. They stood holding each other, shaking. The terror of the moment past, adrenaline overloaded their systems. Relief was flooding their emotions.

"You're an idiot, you know," she started.

"I couldn't let him . . ." the thought trailed off.

"What did you think you were going to do?"

"I didn't know. I just couldn't sit by and do nothing." After a minute he said, "You seemed to do pretty well. I'm not sure you needed me. Oh. Remind me not to make you mad."

"God! I was so relieved to see you. Scared, but happy. And, I couldn't have done anything if you hadn't come – well, and brought the police. I could have gotten away for a bit, but I'm out here alone. He wouldn't take all that, give up, and head back to town for a beer. He would have hunted me down."

"Nice work, young lady," she heard officer Hawkins say. "I'd say he'll be a bit more thoughtful before he accosts another woman. Not that he'll have the chance – at least for a few decades. He was threatening to sue. A minute ago. We got the whole thing on body cam."

"Really glad you got here," said Will. "I'm not sure just what I was going to do."

"Yeah, all's well that ends well," said the officer.

"Shakespeare – nice."

"Well, we all have hidden skills and knowledge – apparently," continued the officer. "I need to get you two back to the parking area. We'll record your statements. You can sign them later. Technically, I'm supposed to separate you two, but I can see that might pose some difficulty."

They walked to the parking area, Shannon and Will with arms around each other. When they reached the area, Sheri ran to Shannon and almost knocked her over. "Oh, god! I was so scared! I was so scared! Are you okay?"

"Yes. I think I'm okay."

Sargent Hawkins walked up. "Okay, Ma'am, if you'll have a seat in our SUV, Officer Phillips will record your statement. Then, we need to get you to the medical center for an examination. Sorry, it's pretty much a legal requirement."

"I can take her," said Will.

"That'll be okay as long as you make sure you get there – directly from here." Then, looking at Will, "We need your statement, too."

"Right with you."

One of the officers was finishing up with Sheri's statement. Sergeant Hawkins escorted Will to the van. On the way, he leaned toward Will, who heard him say, "So, what was your plan?"

"I don't know. I just know I couldn't let him hurt her. Get as close as I could, maybe. Make him come at me with the knife."

The officer interviewing Shannon walked up and said that after the medical exam, somebody should stay with her.

"Sheri and I will likely arm wrestle for the job."

They recorded Will's statement. He wanted to leave out certain things he had done that seemed ill considered, but in the end, he didn't leave anything out. Will, Sheri, and Shannon drove to the medical center, despite Shannon's protestations that she was really okay. The staff took her to a room immediately. While she was being examined, Will drove Sheri to the library, where she retrieved her car. By the time Will and Shannon returned to Shannon's house, Sheri was waiting.

"You'd think I'd just been on a moon mission, or something, the way they were poking and prodding. AND, they made me promise to see this psychologist on Wednesday."

"You've had a traumatic experience," said Will. "The medical tests were to be sure you are okay – and to be used in his trial, if necessary. The psychologist will help with any emotionally traumatic issues. It's for the best. Really."

Sheri returned from the kitchen with a cup of tea. "Here. This will help."

"No. Really. I'm okay."

"Just drink the tea and relax."

Shannon drank her tea. She talked about how Robert had been waiting outside the library. With a knife. She'd used her pepper spray, but that only seemed to infuriate him. He'd grasped her arm – and bruised it – while he tried to clear his eyes. Then, he'd forced her into his car and drove out of town. He had been making delusional statements the entire time. Will described how Shannon had thrashed Robert. Soon, Shannon seemed to tire. She fell asleep on Will's shoulder.

"You might as well carry her to her room," said Sheri.

"I don't want to wake her."

"You won't. I doped her. Stuff they gave me at the medical center. I knew she wouldn't take it on her own. Oh, I'm spending the night. I'll be here on the couch. I have an idea she'd rather wake up next to you than wake up next to me. Go!"

Will lifted Shannon and carried her to the bedroom. He placed her gently on the bed and called for Sheri. "Could you, um, get her into something more comfortable. I don't want to..."

"Even after you two spent the night – you know – best two out of three?"

"That was different. She can't give me permission now. It doesn't seem right."

"There should be more men like you. Oh yeah, this just confirms what she didn't tell me about last night. Way to go! Now all I need are the details."

Will just shook his head and left the bedroom for a few minutes. When he returned, Sheri was tucking Shannon in. "I'll be on the couch. You can hop in next to her. I'm sure she will want something warm and strong to hold on to if she wakes during the night."

Sheri left. Will stripped down to his t-shirt and shorts, then he crawled into the bed. He lay awake watching Shannon sleep, amazed at her beauty and thankful that she was safe.

Forty-six

The smell of cooking bacon awakened Will. Shannon was still fast asleep, so he slid carefully out of bed and pulled on his trousers. He walked to the kitchen and found Sheri at work over the stove.

"Smells good. Good enough to wake the dead."

"Well, thankfully, we don't have to do that. But you see I'm a woman of many talents. If you happen to run across any eligible bachelors, I'm taking applications. Of course, not just anyone will do."

Will was about to say something when Shannon meandered into the room. "I must have been more tired than I thought."

"Well, getting kidnapped at knifepoint will do that to a girl," said Sheri. As she sat Shannon down, she shook her head in a 'no' gesture warning Will not to tell Shannon about the medication. Sheri got Shannon, then Will, each a cup of coffee. "Sorry, no Danish." Will just smiled.

Sheri kissed Shannon on the top of the head. "I know how you like your breakfast, dear." Then, to Will, "Eggs?"

"Please." Sheri tilted her head to the side and gave Will that look. "Over easy, if I could."

"Toast and bacon, too?"

"Yes, please."

"Fine. My pleasure. AFTER, you tell us just where you get the damn Danish."

"Fine. There's a little bakery on Oak. Used to be Betty's. I talked to them. Got a few recipes from a guy I know in Paris. And the secrets, too. Gave them to the owners – they seem nice – in return for free Danish – for you, me, and Shannon. They changed the name to Chez Nous. Happy?"

"I have my moments," Sheri responded, then "one breakfast, coming up."

Breakfast finished, Will cleaned up the dishes and the kitchen. As he did so, Sheri whispered to Shannon, "This guy may be worth keeping. Wonder if he has a brother."

Will finished with the clean-up and sat with a second cup of coffee.

"So," started Shannon, "now that we have the kidnapping out of the way, can I ask where your story is?"

"Sure. I think I've got it pretty much figured out. Ten years ago, or so, there were three guys who worked for a carny. Two brothers, Sam and Phil Russell, were twins, or close enough to be twins. They were pretty well worthless and had joined the carny trying to find a quick and easy way to make some money. Turned out to be more work than they wanted. The manager was about to fire them when they left. They took with them a guy named Riley Tasker. Tasker was pretty good on a motorcycle. His act was to ride around the inside of a twenty-foot sphere – up, down, and around. He had a girlfriend, name unknown, who was supposed to stand inside the sphere during the act."

"Jesus!"

"Yeah. I think that's what she said. All it took was one practice and she took off. Tasker became another roustabout – laborer. So, the two Russell's and Tasker headed out. The Russell boys may have convinced him to leave. Somewhere, they got the idea for this jump and got Tasker to go along. They would get three identical suits for the motorcycle jump. One of the Russell boys would go out, sign autographs, schmooze with the crowd, then disappear into the tent. Tasker, in an identical suit, would make the jump, with his helmet on so nobody could tell it wasn't Russell. On the other side, the bike would be stopped by a pile of cardboard boxes. Tasker would stay in the pile of boxes and the second Russell boy would take the bows. They pick one unknown name, Jake Hughes, because they want it to look like one person, not three.

"Why? Why would Tasker agree to that?"

"My guess is he was better with the motorbike than with business plans, schmoozing with the crowd, or making money. They probably convinced him that the scheme would be a moneymaker for all of them. They kept the spectators on the launch side of the jump – always – and Tasker was probably supposed to crawl out from under the boxes and into a vehicle parked behind the rock outcropping. Only reason to have the jump there. And, remember they only made gap jumps. Spectators were never allowed on the landing side. They cited danger and insurance issues."

"Yeah. That makes sense," said Shannon, "but he didn't make the jump. He plotzed."

"Yeah, that brings me to the ugly part. After the first jump, they made a lot, and I mean a lot more money on later jumps."

"Everybody wants to see a crash," said Shannon quietly.

"Tasker must have known how fast he'd have to leave the ramp to complete the jump. I think one or both of the brothers tampered with the speedometer to make Tasker believe he had the speed when he didn't. They were looking forward to a bigger payday."

"So, they injured him . . ."

"I think they killed him. Seventy-five miles an hour into jagged rocks."

"But he was in the hospital later."

"Well, somebody was in the hospital – rather more of a nursing home. Bandaged. With bandages around the face – I think to hide the identity. They had all their own medical personnel – if they actually were. Where was this so-called survivor treated before he came to the SNF? They would have taken blood, x-rays. There would have to be some trail."

"So, you're saying they killed this man, Tasker, and got rid of the body."

"Big area, Snakebite Canyon."

"Faked the medical stuff, then, what, got somebody else to make the later jumps?"

"They probably sold it to the next guy as a colossal blunder on the part of the first guy. The next guy probably did his own check of the motorcycle. But, from then on, the money was much better."

"But they stopped doing the jumps a few years later," said Shannon.

"Right. Remember, there were rumors that he was killed in Hawaii."

"But there are pictures of him getting off the plane."

"Yes, but suppose one of them was killed in Hawaii. Now, you don't have the duplicate on the far side of the jump. The plan won't work. The sole remaining brother, whichever it is, needs to do something else. He uses his fame to start promoting, which has been very successful."

"Holy crap!" said Sheri. "It all makes sense. How did you . . ."

"That story about the two twins, the girls, switching places. In one of the pictures of a later jump, I was able to find a small figure in a motorcycle suit on the far side of the canyon – before the jump."

"So, how do you prove it?"

"I can't. The authorities could issue some warrants or subpoenas, based on suspicions. We can print the story. It might get some traction. Otherwise, they got away with murder. In my mind, anyway."

The phone rang. Will picked it up. He listened for a few minutes then said, "Thank you. I appreciate the information." He turned toward the ladies. "That was Sergeant Hawkins. They've interrogated Robert. He doesn't do well under pressure. He admitted everything he did yesterday. Wrote it out and signed it. Then, the detectives found an old .22 caliber bullet and told him it was the one from your tire and it matched a test fire from his rifle. And, he confessed to that. When they said they were going to check the rock thrown through your window for finger prints, he told them not to bother, and confessed to that. The detectives were having trouble keeping up typing his confessions. They figure he could get forty years. But, with the confessions, they'll let him off in about two, maybe three decades. You don't have to worry about Robert anymore."

Sheri and Shannon sighed. Then, Shannon said, "Doesn't that seem . . ."

"Like about what he deserves?" finished Sheri.

Forty-seven

Sheri called in and in an uncharacteristic show of support, Lucy said it would be okay if Shannon and Sheri took the day off. Along with Will, they spent the day lounging. Dinner was at a small restaurant downtown.

Sheri felt Shannon was recovering well enough that she would head home to her place for the night. Sheri handed Will the medication to help Shannon sleep.

"If you give her some of this, I expect you not to take advantage."

Will just gave her a disapproving look.

Sheri smiled and slid out the door.

Shannon came up behind Will. "You can give me the meds."

"Wha .. ?"

"Please. I've never conked out like that in my life – without assistance. Give me the meds. I'm not sure I trust you with them."

Will gave her a faux hurt look. Then, he handed over the bottle of pills.

"There. Now I don't need to worry about falling asleep prematurely. And, if you take advantage, at least I'll be able to enjoy it." She said the last with a smile.

"Well, I hadn't really planned on ..."

"Pity," Shannon cut him off, "because this peach is ready to be picked."

They enjoyed a glass of wine, then headed to the bedroom.

Forty-eight

Shannon awoke to hear Will in the shower. She stretched and then curled. They'd spent the night, well most of it, enjoying slow, passionate love. Shannon shivered with joy. She felt totally satisfied. Life, truly, was good.

After his shower, Will dressed. He said he needed to get clean clothes from the hotel. He was also going to stop at Chez Nous for Danish and he would meet both she and Sheri a little later at the office.

Shannon pulled herself from bed. She'd decided that apart from the bruise, her ordeal with Robert had left her pretty much unscathed. She was thankful for that. It could have been so much worse. She removed her clothes and before showering looked at herself in the full-length mirror. *Maybe not over the hill quite yet.*

She emerged from the bathroom in a robe, her hair wrapped in a towel. Will was just finishing his coffee.

"I have a question," she started.

"Yes?" he smiled. "But if it is what I think, we need to get another 'lifetime supply.' We used up the one you say Sheri got you."

Shannon smiled. "Um, that wasn't the question. Not that I'm opposed."

"So?"

"Forgive me from saying so, but it was stupid – maybe a bit strong – if heroic to confront Robert like you did. Not that chivalry isn't appreciated, but I want to know why? You could have waited for the police. It would have been smarter."

"Smarter wasn't in the equation. Only you."

"But he might have had a gun. You might have been killed."

"Didn't matter."

"What!?"

Will paused, stared out the window for a minute, then said, "I guess I can tell you. The truth."

Shannon saw sadness on his face. She wanted to know his

truth, but she felt guilty that she'd been the cause of his sadness. The sadness spread to her.

"I told you I worked for a big paper – after my small paper gig. The larger paper was almost a journalist's dream job. There was a woman. Ariel. We were in love. We were going to be married." He turned from her and faced the window again. "I was on an upward trajectory. And, I guess I was impressed with myself." He turned back toward her. "I got an assignment to cover issues with the Basques – on the border between France and Spain. Ariel – like someone else I've met recently – was hard-headed."

Despite herself, Shannon stuck her tongue out at him.

"After a fair amount of back and forth, I agreed she could come with me – we paid for her travel and stuff, but she was going to have to stay in town while I tried to meet with the rebels – revolutionaries, whatever."

"We stayed in a small hotel in this little town. I got in touch with an intermediary – set up a meeting with the rebels. They agreed because they thought publicity in an American paper would be good for their cause."

"So, one morning, I headed out, accompanied by this guy. Four hours later, we approached the camp. I was searched, and when they were satisfied that I was who I said I was, they allowed me to interview them. It took the day, there were twenty of them, and I stayed the night. Early the next morning, somebody came into camp – excited as hell. It seems they had a car bomb they'd planned to use to blow up the local police station. Somebody screwed up, and it had gone off prematurely – two blocks from the station."

"Oh, no!" It was Shannon.

"I went back to the town as fast as I could. When I got there," he paused. A minute went by. Then, two.

"I found the hotel had been pretty much destroyed. Ten killed. Including the person I'd hoped to keep safe."

"Oh God! Oh, no!"

"The only thing the rebels talked about when they walked me

out was how mad they were about the loss of the explosives and how hard it was going to be to get more. The destruction – the innocent lives – those didn't matter."

Shannon sat looking shocked.

"At first, there was denial. I told myself Ariel was probably out shopping when it happened. Then, they asked me to identify her body. What was left of it. She had been in the restaurant, at the front, when the bomb went off. After denial came despair. My life – the life we'd planned together – was gone."

Shannon started to get up, to go to him, but he held up his hand.

"Despair became anger. All they could think about was getting more explosives. And trying again."

"Two days later, the police raided their camp. I'm pretty good at reconstructing a route, even when blindfolded."

"I wrote a story. Not the one they had wanted. I showed them to be an ill-prepared, ignorant mob of malcontents who would destroy the country if they succeeded. Everyone turned against them, and their cause died. Their leader was captured and jailed for life."

"The pen is mightier than the sword."

He turned to look at her.

"Edward Bulwer-Lytton. Sorry."

"After that," he continued, "I headed to the Middle East and into the areas where there was the heaviest fighting. I told my paper it was to get the best stories. Probably, I just wanted to get myself killed. But I also concentrated on the job. I figured if I got killed, it wouldn't matter, but I wasn't going to put myself in a position to have my heart ripped out again. So, from then on, it's been the job. Only the job. First and foremost."

Shannon was crying.

"Then you came along. And there was Robert."

"But," she said.

"Nobody else dies because of me," he finished. Then, with

everything drained from him, Will collapsed into a chair. "The news agency I work for now found me on the front lines. How? I don't know. But they offered me a job – and a fair amount of counselling. I made my job my life." His demeanor changed, "Until this beautiful redhead shot me with her water – er – soda cannon."

Shannon laughed through her tears and wiped them from her face as she ran to the chair and threw herself on top of him.

Forty-nine

Will Daniels entered the library about 10 AM. He took the stairs two at a time, a bag of Danish and coffee in is hand. When he got to Shannon's office, Sheri was in one of the chairs. Shannon looked upset.

"What's going on?" he asked.

Shannon looked up with red eyes. She handed him a note. "Clode," she said. "God, I hate that woman."

Will took the note. It said, 'Time off is over. The boss wants you to call. He has an assignment. It is urgent.'

Will dropped into the second of Shannon's arm chairs. He was stunned. He knew this would be over sometime, maybe sometime soon, but he didn't want it to be today.

"She probably begged to be the one to break the news," said Shannon.

Will hadn't heard. His eyes refused to focus. His heart pounded in his head.

"You can use my phone," said Sheri.

"Wha...?"

"You can use my phone," repeated Sheri.

"Yeah. Okay."

Will walked to Sheri's office. He was in a daze. He misdialed the first time, then tried again. The phone rang four times in Paris before Clode picked it up.

"Weelyum. How nice of you to call. I guess you received ..."

"Lemme talk to him."

"Weelyum. Don't you want to ..."

"No. I want to talk to him."

The phone clicked to 'hold.'

Will looked across the hall to Shannon sitting behind her desk. She was staring at him. Her face held no emotion.

The phone clicked. "Daniels?"

"Yeah."

"Sorry to cut anything short you might be working on, but we need you. I wouldn't have called – well, I guess Claudine called – if it hadn't been important. I got nobody and the Pope decided he wanted to tell what his plan was to deal with wayward priests. He's telling us – and we – I – need somebody who can do the job right. Got to have you on the plane back here tomorrow night. Again, sorry. I'll try to make it up. You want to talk to Claudine?"

"No." He hung up. He sat staring for five minutes. Shannon got up from her desk and headed to the ladies' room.

He was sitting in her office with Sheri when Shannon returned about twenty minutes later.

Shannon sat in her chair, back straight. She was trying to put on a brave face, but she was having a lot of trouble. But then he thought, *So am I.*

Shannon looked at him in the eyes and said, "When."

"Tomorrow night."

"You cut your hand and put on a really sticky bandage. Time comes to take it off. You do it fast or slow?"

"The faster the better. Hurts less."

"Yeah. Me too. Then, you should give me a kiss and head out. Prolonging this will just ..." and she started to cry.

Will went to her, put his arms around her, and kissed her.

"Go. Go now, please."

Will turned as he walked out the door. Shannon was watching him, tears running down her face.

Fifty

Shannon sat, if you would call it that, in a little ball on her couch. Her head rested against Sheri's shoulder. Sheri had been there all night, cocooning Shannon with her arms and body. Sheri rubbed her arm softly, not knowing what to do to ease Shannon's pain. She knew better than to tell her it would be okay. Shannon's eyes were red and swollen from crying. Inside, there was a giant hand crushing her heart.

"Tennyson was wrong, that bastard. I'd like to wring his neck."

"He's already dead," whispered Sheri.

"I hope it was painful."

"I'm sure it was. Why don't you splash some water on your face? It'll help. Trust me."

Reluctantly, Shannon pulled herself up and headed for the bathroom. Sheri was hoping there would be something she could do to help her friend. Unfortunately, she knew sometimes, pains, especially of the heart, just needed to run their course.

"Sweetie, I'm going to see what's on TV." Sheri stretched as she reached for the remote. She was stiff and sore from being curled around Shannon on the couch all night, but that's what friends do. She hoped TV would provide some distraction.

Shannon returned as the screen came to life.

"And, we're expecting rain this afternoon. Maybe some strong thunderstorms."

"Great," said Shannon, "just what we need. More happy weather."

The screen switched. A man was standing in front of an office building with a microphone in his hand. A red banner at the bottom of the screen flashed 'Breaking News.'

"We now go to Trace Billings in Modesto, California for this breaking news. Trace?"

"That's right. We're standing in front of the offices of Jake Hughes, promoter and former motorcycle daredevil. As you may remember, Mr. Hughes began his career as a motorcycle stunt-man, his stunts almost exclusively canyon jumps. About ten years ago, his first jump was a failure and he fell seventy-five feet into a rocky canyon. After a miraculous escape from major injury, Mr. Hughes returned to make eight more jumps over a period of four years. Then, he began his promotional efforts, which have been very, very successful."

"This morning, search warrants were served on Mr. Hughes' office and home. Mr. Hughes is currently at police headquarters being interviewed. While we're not completely sure what this is about, we have learned through a confidential source that based on information uncovered by the Northern Coloradoan which is due to be published later today, authorities now suspect that Mr. Hughes career started with the death of the person who was actually riding the motorcycle at" the reporter looked down at a paper in his hand, "Snakebite Canyon in Colorado. They apparently believe the motorcycle was tampered with and the death was not accidental. That motorcycle has been kept in a display case here at the Hughes office and we did see the motorcycle removed by forensic officials. If this turns out to be true, this will be a shocking surprise for a very successful career and fans of Mr. Hughes. Back to you."

"Thank you, Trace. We look forward to updates." The newscaster started to shuffle papers on his desk.

Sheri took the remote and turned off the television. "Son of a . . . He gave the story away. A huge story that might have made him famous or . . . He gave it to a small-town weekly. Why?"

Between sobs, Shannon said, "Because on top of everything else, he's a good guy. He knew Julius Frank had been working on this for years and wanted to give him the credit." The rest was lost in sobs.

Shannon curled into an even tinier ball. Sheri put her arms around her and thought, *This is going to take a lot longer than I thought.*

Fifty-one

Will Daniels sat in the terminal of Denver airport. The sun was on its downward trajectory. His flight from Denver to Heathrow would take all night. He would arrive in time for lunch the following day. The plan was to have lunch in London then take the Eurostar back to Paris and his apartment.

He felt terrible. Almost hungover, although he hadn't had any alcohol in a few days. He hadn't slept. When he wasn't tossing and turning, he had a dream about being stranded on a desert island. There were no trees, no food, and no drinkable water. Sun-baked and parched, he watched himself grow older, the sun and elements taking their toll until he was a burned, wrinkled old man. He kept working on little meaningless things as he aged and burned in isolation. A barren existence, with nothing to show for it and no joy.

"British Airways announces the boarding of flight 218 to London's Heathrow airport. Club World passengers are invited to board at this time."

Will picked up his carry-on and headed to the kiosk. He was second in line.

"Welcome to flight 218, Mr. Daniels. We hope you enjoy the flight."

Will thanked the gate representative and headed down the jetway. At the entrance to the plane, he showed his boarding pass to the flight attendant, a young man named Jeremy, who indicated that the Club World seats were to the left.

Seat was actually a misnomer. The Club World passengers had tiny cubicles of their own. The comfortable seat slid down to convert into a bed. Passengers could raise partitions between themselves and their fellow passengers – privacy for sleeping, or just privacy.

Will tossed his carry-on into the overhead and sat down into his seat. He closed his eyes. No matter what he tried, he couldn't get the picture of Shannon out of his head. He heard a quiet, "Ahem." When he opened his eyes, there was a flight attendant standing in the aisle holding a glass of champagne. She had pale skin, freckles, and red hair. Her nametag read Caitlin.

"God. You don't give a guy a break, do you?"

"Sir?" Caitlin seemed authentically puzzled and maybe a bit distressed.

"Nothing. You just remind me of someone – someone I'm leaving behind. Where are you from, Caitlin?"

"I'm sorry you're leaving someone behind. It seems to distress you. I'm from Dublin – Ireland." From the Irish lilt in her voice, Will couldn't ever have mistaken where this young woman was from.

"Well, thank you, Caitlin. I'm sorry if I upset you. It's just, well, the last thing I expected was a beautiful redhead handing me champagne."

"No problem, sir. If there is anything I can do to make your trip easier or more enjoyable, please let me know." Then, she was off, tending to her duties.

Will sipped the champagne, lay his head back, and closed his eyes. Tomorrow, he told himself, this would all be just a memory. He'd be back to his work. Back to things to do.

Fifty-two

The landing gear thumped into place as the Air France Airbus approached Charles de Gaulle Airport in Paris. Will slumped in his seat watching the landscape drift by his window.

"Madames et monsieurs, s'il vous plait . . ."

He checked his seat back and seat belt. He had taken off from Rome just under two hours ago. The flight was on schedule. He was fatigued. Visits to Rome usually cheered him and he would have stayed for a meal, maybe a long walk around part of the city. Today, all he could think about was his apartment and sleep.

His mind drifted to the last few days.

His flight from the United States had arrived in London three days ago. Heathrow was always busy, but he'd come to love London almost as much as Paris, and lunching in London – he hoped – would revive him. He caught the Tube, or Underground, to get to London's West End. He'd stopped at Piccadilly Circus and decided to walk to Leicester Square and a wine bar he was particularly fond of.

He'd stopped at the statue of Eros, although the statue was actually of Eros's brother Anteros, the Greek God of requited love. It was said that if you profess your love by the statue at midnight, you would be rewarded with the eternal love of the one you were with. As he gazed at the statue – for longer than he ever had before – he'd wondered if the story were true. He hoped so. He thought of Shannon.

He entered the wine bar and was greeted by name. His favorite wine was delivered quickly and he ordered lunch. It was nice to be 'home.' Familiar surroundings and people who knew his name. *No rattlesnakes to bite me here*, he'd thought. Then, a hollowness he didn't want to acknowledge grew inside him.

The trip from London to Paris on the Eurostar was routine. He'd arrived in Paris at Gare de Nord. It was a quick Metro ride to his apartment, near the Seine and the two small islands, one which held the cathedral of Notre Dame du Paris. He walked to his building and entered the lobby using his key. The building manager was cleaning the lobby and the entrance to the internal garden. His name was Maurice, and he greeted Will warmly, saying that he had been missed while he was gone. Will's luggage had been delivered and placed into his apartment. Maurice was one of the reasons he loved this place. Maurice was a friend.

Will took the tiny elevator to the top floor and entered the apartment. The décor was modern – streamlined. Clean. His luggage had been placed in his entryway. He carried it to the bedroom, then returned to the living room and opened one of his large windows. He went to his wine closet and retrieved a bottle of burgundy. In his kitchen, he retrieved some brie from the refrigerator. He also made a small salad. For a fee, Maurice would stock the refrigerator with perishables when Will indicated he was returning. It was a luxury he'd grown used to. He smiled. Frequently, Maurice would 'forget' to charge him for the service.

Will carried the refreshments to the small table in front of the sofa. The sounds of the street wafted up and into the apartment. He turned on music. It played so softly he could barely hear it over the noise of the street. This was his refuge. He recharged here, although, today he felt tired and lonely. Worn out – he credited it to his travel, he showered and went to bed early. He awoke early, searching in his half-waking state for someone who wasn't there.

The meeting at the office had been short. His editor told him he was scheduled to meet with the Pope the following day – 10 AM. He handed Will plane tickets for an afternoon flight out of Charles de Gaulle to Leonardo de Vinci. The return was for the following day. There was also a hotel reservation. The Pope was giving the interview to a small group of journalists to lay out his plans for dealing with wayward priests. There would be an interpreter – Will sighed in relief. His Italian left a lot to be desired. Claudine volunteered to go along – her Italian was flawless, she said. Will declined, and Claude pouted.

The meeting with the pontiff started on time and was relatively short. After the formal presentation, sufficient time was allotted for questions and clarification. He'd asked a few questions and gotten a great story. Meeting the Pope was an added plus. As he left Vatican City, he'd called his editor and given him a summary. He would write it up on the flight back to Paris. He should have felt elated – another great story. But he was feeling flat.

The plane landed in Paris and taxied to the terminal. Will grabbed his bag and waited to exit the aircraft. There was no need to head to baggage claim, he'd only brought a carryon. He left the concourse and in the lobby was a chauffer holding a sign with his name on it. The driver introduced himself and led Will to a luxury Peugeot sedan. Claudine was in the back seat waiting for him. She handed him a glass of champagne.

"Claudine, this is supposed to be work."

"This is France – Paris to be exact. There are many ways to work. I could show you."

"Claudine, 'we' are not to be. You should find someone who will appreciate who you are. I'm just not the man…"

"It is her, is it not? The American woman? But she is half a world away. As long as you are here and she is there, why not see if I would be just as desirable – or more?"

He realized how much he missed Shannon and that he had no interest in anyone else. "We are not going to work. Please! Just give it up." *Work. I need to concentrate on work.* But he knew he had a feeling in his heart that he'd buried for so long in fear – the joy that comes with being intimately connected with another.

Mercifully, the drive to the office took only a short time. Will delivered the story to the editor who breezed through it quickly.

"Excellent. Good stuff. It'll be in tomorrow's edition. Listen, you've been traveling and working. You look tired. Why not take a couple of days and do something you really like? You don't really take vacations, and you've earned one. Start small. How about four days? Just kick back. Do something that makes you happy."

Fifty-three

Shannon pulled into her parking spot and turned off the engine. She sat thinking about the day she'd found some stranger had parked there and had been so incensed. Now, she wished she could do it all over again. *Well, maybe not the part with Robert.* She got out of her car and headed into the library. The day was gloomy. She thought maybe the whole world might be gloomy.

Shannon entered her office and immediately looked at the small storeroom/library that Will had used as his office when he was here. The room was dark, deflating her even more. She heard the door behind her and turned expectantly. It was Sheri.

"Hi. How you doing?"

"How do you think? I feel terrible."

"Yeah, well I'm afraid I'm not going to make it any better. Lucy wants to meet with me – now. I have an orientation I'm also supposed to give, in the auditorium, and Lucy said you could handle it for me. I'm sorry. I know it completes your day." Sheri handed Shannon her notes. "The slides are already loaded." Sheri headed out the door, turned and said, "Really. I'm sorry."

Tears rolled down Shannon's cheeks. She just wanted to hide for the morning – maybe the day. Now, she'd have to face a hundred or more faces, eager to start their college careers. Some more eager than others, she had to admit. Hers, she thought, was going to be the least eager of all.

Shannon walked to the auditorium and entered one of two doors at the lectern level. The seats were tiered upward, with two sets of stairs leading from the entrance in the lobby down to the lectern level effectively spitting the seats into three sections. The lectern level was elevated a foot above the floor. Her guess had been correct. There were about a hundred bodies in the seats. The lights were dimmed.

"Good morning. My name is Shannon Sullivan. I am the assistant director of library services here at the university. You folks seem to be spread out. I think if you could move down – closer to the front, you would be able to see better and hear me better." No one moved. No surprise. The cynical part of Shannon thought, *Is this an audience or a photograph?*

"Okay. As I mentioned, I am the ..."

A student, young man, got up from his seat in the upper left wing and started down the stairs.

Well, at least one is moving.

"I am the ..."

But the student didn't stop when he got to the bottom of the stairs. He walked directly to where Shannon was standing behind the lectern, smiled a very slight smile, and handed her a single long-stemmed red rose. Then, he turned and walked out the door Shannon had entered.

"Um ..." was all Shannon could get out while she watched him exit. She shook her head and was about to speak when she saw another student, a young woman, get up from her seat in the upper center, and descend the stairs on the right. Like the first student, she walked directly to Shannon and handed her a single long-stemmed red rose. Then, like the first student, she exited the auditorium through one of the lower doors.

Before Shannon could even begin to process this, students, one by one all began to make their way to where Shannon was standing. Then, they came two at a time, the next student moving when the first was half-way down the stairs. Then, they came three at a time. None said a word, but all handed her a single long-stemmed red rose. In ten minutes, Shannon was standing alone in the auditorium, one hundred long-stem red roses overflowing the lectern.

A lone figure emerged from the very dark upper left corner of the room and made his way down the stairs. Will Daniels, in university sweatshirt and jeans, walked up to the stage. He handed Shannon a flower. It was a single stem with two perfect rose blossoms on it.

"As it turns out, my world without you is very dark, desolate, and lonely. My world with you in it is bright and filled with joy." Will got down on one knee and opened a small box containing a large diamond engagement ring. "It is my most sincere wish that your world and my world will become our world. I'd love to spend the rest of my life worshiping you – having you as my wife. I promise I will do everything I possibly can to make you happy."

Shannon jumped off the stage, knocking Will over. She was on top of him, her arms around him, squeezing him and showering him with kisses.

"I'm hoping that was a yes."

"Yes! Yes! Yes!" Then, after a very passionate kiss, Shannon smiled and said, "Yes, I will allow you to do everything possible to make me happy." They both laughed and kissed again.

In the projection booth, two figures watched. "Thanks, Lucy. I couldn't have done it without you."

"I don't know what you're thanking me for, Sheri. I have an idea your workload just doubled."

Fifty-four

Shannon lay face down on the massage table completely naked. To her right, sheer curtains allowed the passage of light through the wall of windows but kept at bay any prying eyes. The sounds of Paris drifted up from four stories below.

"I'm a puddle. You did this to me." Her voice was just above a whisper.

Will sat in a bistro-type chair. He'd given Shannon a two-hour, head-to-toe massage. He finished by wiping the massage oil from her with a wet and hot – almost, but not quite, too hot – cloth. "I just wanted you to be relaxed."

"Relaxed isn't the word for it. What if there's a fire?"

"I'll put a robe around you and carry you to safety." He drew his fingers down her spine from neck to derriere.

"Oooooo. That isn't helping. And by the way, the massage was great – I mean all of it. You said you had classes?"

"Yes. I took some classes. I hope you approve."

"Approve doesn't cover it, BUT halfway through when you did your tongue massage on and in my ... Was that part of the class as well?"

"Um, no. That, my love, was reserved for you and you only."

"Uh huh."

Shannon felt a playful slap on her bottom followed by a soft kiss in the same place.

"What a naughty man you are, titillating a woman with a spank then exciting her with a kiss on her bottom."

"And, which is the naughtier? The man doing the deed or the woman who has to admit that it was indeed titillating and exciting?"

"And doing it to a married woman, as well."

"I am lucky enough to be married to the goddess I will worship until the end of my life."

"Well, I'd better find some way to move from here. We have to pick Sheri up at the airport in two hours."

"I could give you a complete bath while you lie there. You wouldn't have to move for a bit."

"I wouldn't be able to move for days. Did you hear me about Sheri?"

"Françoise is picking up Sheri."

"Françoise? They did seem to hit it off when she was here a few months back."

"Yes. So much so that he flew to see her a month ago."

"She never told me. Why that little ..."

"Françoise said he would pick her up but then he had to stop at his place. Something he had to do."

"Something or someone?"

"Madame, you are so suspicious. He said they are stopping for coffee. Anyway, we will meet them for dinner. It won't be too long, I guess, before she will be staying at his place instead of in our guest room here when she visits."

"Coffee was our code word for sex. So, free until dinner. What shall we do?" She said it with a smile.

Will picked her up and carried her to the bed a few steps away. "I think I can place kisses on all those beautiful little freckles that cover you everywhere."

"You seem to be very good at one particular spot."

"Then, there is where I will start."

ABOUT THIS BOOK

As stated in the beginning, this is a book of fiction. Characters, places, and events are fictitious or used fictitiously.

Ft. Collins, Colorado is situated approximately seventy miles north of Denver, along the front range of the Rocky Mountains. Colorado State University is located in Ft. Collins and provides a backdrop for the story, although it is used fictitiously and not named as such. Places noted in Ft. Collins are either fictitious or were presented with their names changed. There is no Snakebite Canyon in the area. Unfortunately, the Red Garter After Hours Club does not exist.

Sheri Chapman was a real person and a friend. She was thoughtful, intelligent, caring, and warm. She had a quick mind and great sense of humor. She was a person with whom you could have an intelligent conversation or a good laugh, to whom you could go with a problem, and who would be there if you needed a shoulder to cry on. Her passing has left a void. My hope is that she is looking down smiling at my portrayal of her.

My thanks also to Leo Scully, formerly Air Force security officer and of the District of Columbia Metropolitan Police Department. He kept me from making a few particularly egregious errors in police procedures. Any remaining are mine entirely.

To Tonia and Becky, who I met at the Birchmere, in Virginia, during a Jeff Daniels Band concert, I hope this makes you smile. They asked if there might be a part in a future novel. They are not, by the way, twin sisters. In this case, the activities are completely fabricated. While their husbands asked if they could be written as ladies with loose morals, I hope I've turned the tables and put the joke on the husbands – fictitiously, of course.

Finally, while remaining characters are fictional, if you should be in Paris and see a beautiful red-haired woman on the arm of a distinguished man who appears to be totally in love with her, well . . .

Thank you for reading my book. I hope you enjoyed it.

If you liked this book, <u>please leave a review on Amazon</u>. Reviews help other readers find books they would like to read and help authors improve their own works.

In addition, if you would like to be one of my beta reviewers – someone who reads my books before publication and who receives the completed book free of charge, please send your name and e-mail address to my publisher at TWeaver2008@aol.com to be included in this group.   You may opt out at any time.   You can also contact me through my website https://www.annaleighromance.com/

Books by Anna Leigh

<u>Loves Lost and Found</u> – A Mystery Romance Adventure

<u>Lost in the Forest</u> – A Romantic Wilderness Adventure

<u>River Cruise Undercover</u> – A Romantic Travel Adventure

<u>Rocky Mountain Romance</u>

ABOUT THE AUTHOR

Anna Leigh lives in suburban Maryland. She enjoys musical theater, loves to travel, and cares for small animals. She also enjoys fitness activities and has completed numerous Spartan challenges.

Made in the
USA
Middletown, DE